'Do..

Josh di
small br
the floor.

Karis sat clutching her knees. 'I like him very much, Josh. I like him because he's your daddy and because he has a lovely smile and is very good-looking—almost as good-looking as you,' she teased, and Josh looked up and grinned at her. 'He has been very sad living away from you,' Karis continued. 'I want you to be a family again.'

'I'm happy with you and baby Tara,' the boy murmured, and Karis drew him into her arms. If she could have one wish now it would be to find herself engaged to be married to the little boy's father…

Natalie Fox was born and brought up in London and has a daughter, two sons and two grandchildren. Her husband, Ian, is a retired advertising executive, and they now live in a tiny Welsh village. Natalie is passionate about her cats—two strays brought back from Spain where she lived for five years—and equally passionate about gardening and writing romance. Natalie says she took up writing because she absolutely *hates* going out to work!

A Marriage In The Making

NATALIE FOX

Harlequin Mills & Boon

SYDNEY ❀ AUCKLAND ❀ MANILA
LONDON ❀ TORONTO ❀ NEW YORK
PARIS ❀ AMSTERDAM ❀ HAMBURG ❀ MILAN
STOCKHOLM ❀ MADRID ❀ ATHENS ❀ BUDAPEST
WARSAW ❀ SOFIA ❀ PRAGUE ❀ TOKYO ❀ ISTANBUL

All the characters in this book have no existence outside the imagination of the Author, and have no relation whatsoever to anyone bearing the same name or names. They are not even distantly inspired by any individual known or unknown to the Author, and all the incidents are pure invention.

Published by
Harlequin Mills & Boon
3 Gibbes Street, Chatswood, NSW 2067 Australia

First published in Great Britain 1997
Australian copyright 1997
New Zealand copyright 1997
Philippine copyright 1997
First Australian Paperback Edition 1997

ISBN 0 73350 732 8

Printed and bound in Australia by
Griffin Press, South Australia

CHAPTER ONE

KARIS watched with interest as the *Estrella* slid smoothly alongside the jetty, the oily throb of its engines barely audible over the swish of surf on the white sands of Fiesta's private tropical island.

In the shade and the leafy seclusion of a banyan tree on the edge of the beach, unobserved by anyone on board, Karis gently readjusted baby Tara on her hip as the vacationers started to alight from the yacht.

There were the usual this week: several middle-aged, portly gentlemen in Bermuda shorts with beautiful golden-skinned blondes sashaying along the wooden jetty after them. The more leggy and beautiful the blonde, the richer the portly gentleman, it appeared.

Karis watched them come ashore with a soft smile of amusement on her full lips. There had been a time when she had found it unbearable to watch the disembarking ritual, almost despising those people for coming here to enjoy themselves. They were usually couples and, however ill matched some might appear, they were nevertheless together, which made her feel her own loss so deeply.

It had got easier over the months, though, and now she could watch with amusement instead of envy and irritation. She might not have a partner of her own any more but she had something those leggy blondes hadn't. She had the love of two adorable children, a certain measure of contentment in her life now and Josh had helped her regain her self-worth, which she hadn't possessed when she had arrived a year ago.

And Josh—where was he? Karis turned to see him happily

engaged in trying to entice a land crab out from under a clump of cactus a little way along the deserted beach, so Karis didn't feel guilty for giving the last two passengers left on deck a little more of her curious attention.

He was gorgeous—neither middle-aged nor portly but obviously affluent judging by the cut of his white linen trousers and midnight-blue silk shirt. He was tall, with glossy black hair and dark, broody good looks, and Karis gazed at him in awe for a few seconds and then shifted her dark eyes to the lady with him. She was gorgeous too, as would be expected. Her hair was reddy gold and her flowing silk print outfit was lovely and Karis had to admit she looked rather more intelligent than the usual females who came to the island for fun and sun.

Beautiful people the couple might appear but, alas, beautiful people they didn't sound to Karis, who was totally mesmerised by the charismatic stranger who was speaking now in such a controlled manner to his companion.

'Leave the luggage, Simone,' he ordered firmly. 'There are staff to take care of it and nothing can get lost.'

'I'm not taking any chances,' came back the determined reply—a cutting remark which, to his credit, her companion ignored.

The man, with his eyes hidden by dark sunglasses, stood with his hands gripping the curving rail of the yacht, his jaw set as if in stone, and Karis guessed he was determinedly controlling his impatience and temper. He waited, silently, broodingly, while his companion curtly instructed one of the crew to haul her bags out from under the rest of the luggage *now* and to take it up to the plantation house and deposit it in her suite and nowhere else.

'Honey child,' drawled the good-humoured West Indian, 'I crew this yacht and that's as far as my duties go. You wanna packhorse you—'

'Packhorse at your service, ma'am,' came the cry from Leroy, one of Fiesta's houseboys, as he ran barefoot along the jetty to greet them.

Karis pressed two fingers firmly over her lips to stifle her amusement as she watched the spectacle of Leroy charming and disarming the irascible red-gold lady with his open, honest grin of welcome and his willingness to obey her any command at a moment's notice.

The impressive-looking man with her didn't appear to notice what was going on, the taming of his companion. He was leaning on the rail now, in a world of his own, gazing at the small tropical island, his jawline still rigidly set, his broad shoulders tense and unyielding under the silk of his shirt as it rippled against him in the rush of a tropical breeze. Karis imagined his eyes to be glacier-blue under cover of his heavy sunglasses, because for all his obvious good looks he appeared a cold sort of person and one not particularly pleased to be here.

Karis remembered her own feelings on approaching the island for the first time, on the very same yacht. Her small fists had gripped the rail the same way and the beauty of the small paradise island, set like a precious jewel in a sea of turquoise satin, had gone unregistered by her as it appeared to be by him now. She hadn't been able to appreciate its loveliness because of trepidation at the thought of the new life ahead of her. To have had to come this far across the world to free herself of a past that had caused her such pain had quashed all but anxiety from her senses.

The stranger had a similar look about him—as if he lived with regrets and was doubtful that coming here was a good idea—and Karis was intrigued.

But it was all supposition, Karis mused as she watched the two of them, with Leroy following under a mountain of luggage, walk along the jetty to the beach and the garden path that led to the main house of the island. She couldn't be sure what the stranger was thinking or feeling because she didn't know him, but it was just the overall impression he gave—one of reluctance and withdrawal and not wanting to be here.

Suddenly Josh's warm, sandy hand slipped into hers and she gripped it reassuringly and gave him her full attention now. The small boy was watching the visitors too, his dark, dark eyes unreadable. It had been one of her greatest joys when she had first broken through his reserve and been able to read those dark eyes. It had become a frequent occurrence recently but now they were closed off from her.

'More visitors,' she told him softly. 'No children this time, though.' She gave his hand another reassuring squeeze. The diminutive five-year-old in her care needed the company of other children. She grinned to cover a sigh, not wanting him to pick up on her disappointment. 'You'll have to put up with baby Tara for a playmate for a little longer.'

But Tara wasn't enough for Josh. She was only a tot and not able to communicate with him sensibly. He needed children of his own age and older, not that he mixed all that well when they did come to the island. It usually took him a few days to assess any young visitors tentatively, and by the time they were ready to leave Josh was just about relaxed enough to *try* and make friends. Most of the time Karis felt he was only making the effort to please her anyway. Josh must have been born a loner, she supposed, but she still encouraged him to socialise whenever she had the opportunity.

So, no children this time. If there had been they would have eventually found their way to Karis's cottage where they would have been made welcome. 'Nanny Extraordinaire', was how Fiesta referred to her in her more charitable moments, but most of the time she treated her with indifference. Karis was the hired help, hired to keep Josh out from under her feet.

And Josh was difficult and moody and unresponsive a lot of the time. Like now, as he stared rigidly at the three people coming up the beach towards the plantation house, the male visitor with his hand gently at the woman's elbow in case she stumbled in the deep sand, neither speaking but Leroy making up for it with a cheerful banter of useful and useless information about the island that was apparently falling on deaf ears.

Karis felt stirrings of something she didn't want to acknowledge—that old feeling of envy and regret she used to feel when the laughing, loving couples came happily ashore. These two were hardly love's sweet dream but Karis nevertheless felt a pang or two of envy of the woman with such a heart-wrenching good-looking partner. Cool and aloof he might appear, but he was with her all the same, and courteous and attentive too. They were together, a couple, him and her, here to enjoy a vacation in paradise, and it squeezed at Karis's heart. She had no partner any more, not even one to argue with now and then, and at this moment, for some peculiar reason, she felt her loss more poignantly than usual.

Quickly dismissing such irrational thoughts of envy, Karis stepped forward out of the shade of the banyan, intending to walk along the beach to her cottage with the children. Tara was still asleep against her shoulder and Josh was in need of his siesta, but suddenly the boy's hand tightened in hers and pulled at her, stopping her dead in her tracks. At the same time he let out a peculiar sound from deep in his throat.

The visitors had reached the gardens at the point where they met the beach, and were only twenty metres or so from them when Josh's small cry had the man stopping and jerking his head in their direction.

For some reason Karis's stomach tightened as the others strode on and the man stood stock-still, staring at her with baby Tara on her hip and the small, dark-haired boy, barefoot and brown as a nut as she was, now almost hidden behind her crimson sarong. She felt Josh's fists clawing into the back of her skirt, twisting the cotton print in his anxious small hands.

The man stared and then slowly his hand came up to strip the sunglasses from his face, and in that moment of revelation Karis knew who he was and the muscles of her stomach clenched ever tighter and her heart thundered perilously.

He said not one word. His eyes didn't speak either. They weren't blue at all but a dark, indiscriminate colour that looked as if their hue was gauged by mood. The mood now was cold and hostile as they raked Karis up and down, not settling, not appraising, just coldly grazing over her, making prickles of fear shoot across the surface of her skin.

Josh was stiff behind her, still clutching her skirt, and then Karis felt a tremble shudder through his slim little body. Without taking her green eyes from the stranger, she quickly moved her hand behind her to caress the boy's bare head tenderly and reassure him he was safe with her.

A slight look of puzzlement chased across the man's eyes and then they narrowed, and the look chilled Karis to the bone. Disapproval entered the eyes then as the gaze once again slid over her skimpy vest-top and the tumble of wild, unkempt jet hair that skimmed her brown shoulders. A soft tropical breeze flattened her skirt against her long legs and she felt the thin cotton clinging to her, outlining her shape and making her feel almost naked under his icy scrutiny. But there was nothing sexual in the way he was looking at her, only a chilling disapproval—which oddly felt worse.

Josh nervously moved then. Karis was aware of his bare feet shifting agitatedly in the sand and then, with another small, throaty whimper, he let go of her skirt and started to run, crashing through the lush vegetation behind them and on towards the cottage.

Karis's first instinct was to call out to him, but she stemmed the cry in her throat so as not to alarm Tara. Her small daughter stirred in her arms and Karis wrapped her free hand around the back of her head and held her close, soothing the child back to sleep with her fingers stroking her dark, silky hair.

She never took her eyes off the dark stranger because a peculiar thing had happened to the man's expression. On sight of the defecting child and the sound of his whimper of anguish as he had fled a look of such deep pain had passed over that handsome though rigid face that Karis's pulses raced in turmoil.

'Daniel!'

The piercing cry cut through the hot, humid air, jerking Karis's senses. The stranger didn't respond, his hard, muscle-bound body didn't move a centimetre, but then she supposed he wasn't the sort to jump to such a shrill command from a woman.

Karis stepped back, desperately wanting to break the eye contact between them because it was unnerving her, but it was so hard to do. Curiosity had frozen her at first and then all sorts of emotions had rushed at her and still he stared at her, fixing her to the spot. And how he glared now that Josh had fled in such distress. Was he blaming her for the small boy's terrified reaction? She didn't know. Deep concern for Josh was what finally broke her eye contact with him. She swung round, turning her back on the man she now knew to be Daniel.

She knew who he was and Josh had known him too and Karis's heart squeezed painfully. Still balancing the sleeping baby on her hip, she walked straight-backed along the beach towards the cottage, sensing he was still watching her and helpless to do anything but let the shivers prickle her spine till she was safely out of distance. That cold, cold scrutiny of her had shaken her so deeply and darkly, it seemed as if the sunshine had disappeared for ever. Narrowing her eyes, she had to look up into the blue sky to reassure herself it was still there.

Saffron, the West Indian housemaid, took the sleeping baby from Karis's arms as Karis stepped up onto the wooden verandah of the white coral stone cottage she shared with the two children. She smiled helplessly at Karis and spoke in a lilting whisper so as not to wake Tara.

'He's under the bed, Miss Karis. Making that funny sound again, so vexed it makes your own heart cry out. You've done so well with him and now—'

'He'll be OK,' Karis reassured her, and smiled warmly at Saffron, who had been such a support to her this last year. 'Put Tara down in her cot for me and I'll coax him out, Saffron.'

'I tried already, tempted him with his favourite pumpkin pie, but it's no good; he just yowls and yowls. That child needs a doctor, one of them head doctors—'

'Hush now, Saffron.' Karis laughed softly, knowing she didn't mean it and understanding why she said such things at times like this.

Saffron cared about Josh as deeply as Karis did and when Josh was hurting they all hurt, Saffron's pain manifesting itself more dramatically than Karis's with suggestions of psychiatrists and, once, voodoo!

'You know as well as I do what Josh needs,' Karis added meaningfully.

'Well, he ain't going to get it with that one,' she said, meaning Fiesta and nodding towards the plantation house that was out of sight of the cottage, across the lush tropical gardens. Clutching Tara to her ample breasts, she turned and padded along the verandah, softly crooning to the baby and rocking her gently.

With a soft, long-drawn-out sigh of agreement Karis stepped into the open kitchen, poured herself a glass of water and sipped it slowly to calm herself. No, Josh wouldn't get what he needed from Fiesta—a stable family life. Fiesta was too busy running her lucrative vacation business to give Josh what he needed.

It had always been a mystery to Karis why the boy was in Fiesta's care when it was obvious he wasn't wanted. At first it had crossed her mind that Fiesta might be Josh's mother, but apparently not. No mother could treat a child with so much indifference, even if he had resulted from an unwanted pregnancy or was the product of a broken marriage. Nevertheless Josh *was* in Fiesta's care and even Saffron didn't know why or how. All Saffron knew was that there was a father somewhere but a mother had never been mentioned.

Karis carefully sliced a chunk of Saffron's creamy pumpkin pie and poured a glass of milk for Josh in the kitchen. She carried them on a tray out onto the verandah and along to his bedroom which was next to hers, and firmly dispelled the cloud of depression that was promising to settle if she didn't watch out. Josh needed reassuring and loving and she needed a smile on her face for that.

Karis made no attempt physically or verbally to persuade Josh out from under the bed. Past experience had taught her the task was hopeless. He'd come out when he was ready and she would be there for him, as always. She sat in a cane chair by the open patio doors, the air breezy and sweet with the scent of jasmine, and started to read softly from one of his favourite books, but as she read her mind was drifting elsewhere, reliving that cold, cold glare from the newly arrived stranger.

The man, with his impressive bearing and indisputable good looks, had mesmerised her from her first sight of him, but it hadn't been a pleasant feeling—more disturbing than anything else. He had appeared to be as cold and hard as honed steel and yet that look of pain when Josh had defected…or had she imagined it?

'W…w…w…'

'Deep breaths, Josh,' Karis suggested gently as she put the book down and lifted the boy onto her lap to cuddle him. He'd been standing looking over her shoulder for ages as she'd read but she hadn't let on she knew he was there. It had to come from him otherwise it was hopeless. She held his forehead as he leaned back against her, taking deep breaths as she had suggested.

They had come a long way. A year ago, when Karis had arrived with four-month-old baby Tara, the boy had been silent, refusing to speak except to stutter abuse at Fiesta. Karis had been shocked and deeply upset by his behaviour, and shaken by Fiesta's uncaring attitude towards the troubled boy. It was obvious he was an embarrassment to her in front of her guests and she wanted him out from under her feet and frankly didn't care who unburdened her.

While in England, promoting her exclusive, private Caribbean island holidays, Fiesta had advertised for a nanny and Karis had applied. Though she had no qualifications, Karis had been desperate enough to try for the job. At the interview Fiesta had said nothing about the boy being a problem child. It had only been when Karis arrived on Levos that she'd found out just what a problem he was and, worse, that apparently she was the latest in a long line of nannies, most highly qualified but unable or unwilling to cope with the appalling little boy.

At first Karis had thought she couldn't cope herself, not with Tara and the sadness and tragedy of her own past to come to terms with as well. But something about the badly behaved boy had tugged so painfully at her heartstrings that she hadn't been able to leave. And, strangely, having to care for Josh, having to give so much of herself to gain his confidence, she had found he had unknowingly given her much in return. She had arrived on the island a shadow of her former self, rock-bottom low and with little self-esteem, only to find a very frightened little boy with much the same hang-ups and misery. It had brought her up short. In a child, disturbance and melancholia were all the more tragic. It wasn't natural for a child to be so deeply unhappy.

So Karis had forced her own self-pity behind her, cared for Josh and her own baby daughter, and made life bearable and as much fun as possible for them all. It had been a long, hard, painful haul to win Josh's trust, and there were still days when he was difficult, but on the whole he was a much happier child than he had been a year ago and Karis was no longer the shadow of grief she had been when she had arrived.

'W...will he take me away?' Josh breathed at last.

Karis held him close, smoothing a hand across his hot brow. 'Will who take you away?' she dared to ask, wanting confirmation from him that Daniel was who she thought he was. Fiesta wasn't at all forthcoming about Josh's past. Karis had asked her about Josh's parentage once but a tight-lipped Fiesta had told her to mind her own business and do what she was paid to do: look after the boy.

'My father,' Josh blurted. 'Will he take me away?'

So he *was* Josh's father. She had thought so when he had removed his sunglasses. They had the same eyes—cold and inhospitable, suspicious, cautious...and yet there were times when Josh's eyes showed deep warmth and love and bright humour and perhaps the father had the capability of such emotions in him too. The thought gave a curious twist to her senses.

'I don't know,' Karis admitted truthfully. She was always honest with him because he was too intelligent to be fobbed off with excuses. 'But I'll find out what's going on, Josh,' she promised, hugging the boy to her.

And she would. Daniel Kennedy, Josh's father, was on the island and the reason must be to see his son and discuss his future with Fiesta, for surely he didn't expect the wealthy socialite to look after him indefinitely? And where was Josh's mother? That Simone certainly wasn't his mother because Josh would have said if she was.

It was so worrying to Karis. Caring for him every day of their lives, she knew that the child needed a stable home life, preferably with a full set of parents, and though she had done her best a nanny's best wasn't enough to carry the child through the rest of his childhood. And when he did go? She, with Tara, would have to move on and carve out another new life for them both because they couldn't go back. Karis wouldn't be welcomed back; she didn't want to go back. She'd learnt a lot here—not least that a simple life was worth a king's ransom in terms of peace of mind.

'Can we go to the creek?' Josh asked tentatively. One hand was curved over his shoulder, twisting a strand of Karis's jet hair around his fingers as she cuddled him. The small, intimate gesture of confidence and caring for her always pulled at Karis's heart. She knew that in his way the boy cared very deeply for her and if his father had come to take him away...

It didn't bear thinking about but a small thought stayed around long enough to have Karis grasping at it with both hands. If his intention *was* to take the child off the island he would still need a nanny—unless, of course, there *was* a mother around...but no one knew if one even existed. Both Josh and Fiesta were a closed book where Josh's past was concerned. It was as if he had never lived before his two years on this island.

'Yes, we'll go to the creek,' Karis decided quickly, bear-hugging the boy to her and planting a squidgy kiss beneath his ear, making him laugh.

Daniel might come to the cottage looking for his son but Saffron was here and would tell him where they were. Optimistically Karis imagined telling him all about his estranged son, what a good swimmer he was, how well he could read—

an amazing achievement for a five-year-old who a year ago hadn't been able to string a sentence together.

Yes, she would have so much to tell him, so why was that grey cloud of uncertainty looming? She knew but didn't want to think about it. One day soon, she and Tara would lose Josh to his cold, unfeeling father and... No, she wouldn't think about it, not yet. Josh wanted to swim and dive and chase sea turtles under the water and frankly so did she.

'Are you sure you don't mind staying on while I'm over at the main house, Saffron?' Karis asked later.

Saffron lived over at the staff cottages behind the plantation house and Karis had never had reason to ask her to stay late before. She had no social life and there was certainly nowhere to go on the tiny island even if she had. She had never been issued with an invitation to join one of Fiesta's house parties, of which there were numerous in the holiday season. She was staff after all.

'Of course I don't mind,' Saffron told her as she finished off the washing up and turned to gaze at Karis, who was trying to do something with her unruly hair in front of the kitchen mirror. 'Best if you find out what that boy's father's intentions are.'

'Yes, indeed,' Karis murmured thoughtfully. She coiled her hair in a bundle on the top of her head and secured it with a gilt clasp. She had dressed in her best outfit—a slip of a silk dress in dark green with fine shoulder straps. Her feet were bare, though. After a year of tropical island living shoes and even sandals were unbearable on her feet. She supposed she had gone native this last year but the laid-back lifestyle of the West Indians had appealed to her after the formality of life in Britain. She was freer here than she had ever been before. But she was bowing to convention now, making the best of herself to face Fiesta and possibly Josh's father, because it was important that she give a good impression...but blow the shoes!

'Are you sure Josh's father didn't come to the cottage while Josh and I were along at the creek?' she asked as she tucked an unruly wisp of dark hair back into the clasp.

Earlier she'd told Saffron about Josh's father arriving on the island and had fully expected him to come to the cottage to see his son once he had unpacked. She couldn't believe that he hadn't.

'I'm sure,' Saffron assured her. 'I sat out on that verandah all the time and he didn't come near.'

And yet Karis had been sure they had been watched as they'd swum and practised diving in the tiny creek on the other side of the island, only fifteen minutes' walk away but far enough to claim seclusion. Fiesta's guests were generally a lazy lot who never ventured far from the opulent plantation house with its swimming pool and the bar lavishly stocked with every cocktail ingredient imaginable.

She must have been mistaken, unnerved by that dark man's unyielding eyes as he had stopped and stared earlier, and imagined he must be shadowing her and Josh.

'It's awful,' Karis sighed, and licked her fingers and smoothed them over her dark brows. 'He hasn't seen him at all since I've been looking after him. It's the first time I've seen him.'

'He came when you were on St Lucia with Tara for her check-up, six months ago,' Saffron told her, rubbing her hands on a tea-towel as Karis swung to face her in surprise. 'You remember the boy was yowling for a week when you came back.'

'I thought it was because he was angry with me for not taking him,' Karis stated in astonishment. 'Why didn't you tell me, Saffron?' Oh, she should have done. It would have helped to know the real reason for Josh's distress.

Saffron shrugged without looking at her. 'No good you vexing yourself about it too.'

'Hmm. Maybe.' Karis exhaled. That was Saffron's reasoning—ignorance was bliss—and perhaps she was right. Karis would have vexed herself over it.

She would have liked to know all the same; after all, she was the closest to the small, troubled boy and she might have been able to draw him out if she had known what was bothering him. It dragged at her heart to think the child was in such fear of his own father.

'I won't be long,' she told Saffron from the open door onto the verandah. 'If the children wake—'

'They won't,' Saffron laughed, and then the wide grin drained from her round face and she grew serious. 'I wish you were all dressed up like that for a date.'

'A date with whom?' Karis laughed softly and added teasingly, 'One of those ghastly rich old men that fly down from Miami for Fiesta's vacations? I'd rather court the devil, Saffron.'

'Wicked girl!' Saffron chastised her, with humour softening the remark.

'Not at all a wicked girl,' Karis muttered under her breath as she followed the path to the plantation house through the subtly lit gardens. The devil himself was a safer bet than the one man she'd allowed into her life, the man she had married and lost so tragically. Poor Aiden. Karis shivered sorrowfully in spite of the cloying heat. He hadn't deserved what fate had dealt him, no matter what he had done. But he had given her Tara, the one good thing he had done in his life, and for that she couldn't allow his memory to fade though her memories of him were tinged with sadness and bitterness most of the time.

It was a velvety black tropical night with heavy cloud obscuring the moon and pressing the heat of the day back down to earth, making the air thick and heady. Karis could hear laughter coming from the beach and smell the charcoal grill sizzling T-bone steaks and so she avoided the waterfront route to the house. Fiesta hadn't got her nickname for nothing. She knew how to throw a beach party.

As Karis strolled unhurriedly through the scented gardens she rehearsed in her head what she wanted to say to Fiesta...and Josh's father if he was around. The boy needed so much more than he was getting on the island. He needed proper schooling for one thing, though Karis did her best. She didn't want to lose him, dreaded the thought in fact, but his welfare and future were her chief concern and that small thought she had grasped to her earlier was growing in momentum. If this wasn't just a visit and Daniel was planning on taking Josh back to the States he would need a nanny for him, and who better for the job than the one who had cared for the child and had worked a small miracle on him this last year?

Karis circled the house till she was under the wide wrought-iron balcony of the sitting room, where lights blazed out from the open French doors. She'd checked with Fiesta's housekeeper where she was and rather than go through the house and run the risk of bumping into any of the house guests, who were usually well on the way to being drunk at this time of the night, she had skirted the house and opted for the balcony and the small flight of wrought-iron steps that led up to it from the rose gardens beneath.

'What qualifications has she got?' The brutal query came from above Karis's head and it stilled her instantly. She flattened herself against the scratchy coral wall of the house, under the balcony where it was shadowy and she couldn't be seen. The deep, resonant voice was Daniel Kennedy's and she knew instinctively he was referring to her.

'Qualifications? You expect someone with qualifications to

give your uncontrollable son the time of day? Get real, Daniel. Karis is the only one to have stayed!' Fiesta argued stiffly.

'And it's quite obvious why,' Daniel stated emphatically. 'She's nothing but a child herself, and wild with it—all that hair and barefoot like a native. She must have thought she'd landed on her feet when you offered her this luxurious life. Where the hell did you drag her up from?'

Karis steeled herself, muscles cramping, closing her eyes tightly against the pain of the insult.

'And the baby on her hip,' he ground on, not giving Fiesta a chance to explain. 'I don't expect her to look after other people's children when I'm paying her to look after Josh.'

'Tara is her own child.'

There was a gasp of exasperation from Josh's father. 'It gets worse! You never told me all this the last time I was here.'

'I wasn't going to cook the golden goose, was I? I took her on because she was young and looked capable enough to handle him. Having her own child didn't matter to me. As it turns out Karis is good for the boy.'

'Good for him!' he responded in disbelief. 'Some unkempt teenager with an illegitimate—'

Karis's fiercely clenched fists bunched over her ears to shut the world out. She didn't want to hear any more—she couldn't; it was unbearable.

Hurt beyond measure by that cutting jibe against her, she stealthily crept away from the house and only broke into a shaky trot when she knew she couldn't be heard blundering through the vegetation in the gardens. The suffocating humidity of the night quickly drained her and by the time she reached the beach she was breathless, clutching at her throat for air and ripping the clasp from her hair with her other hand and shaking it wild and free.

Unkempt, was she? Wild, was she? What did *he* know? Just what did *he* know? Tears streamed down her cheeks and with a sob she lifted her face to the soft, warm breeze to dry them. She was hurt and angry—yes, *very* angry.

How could he have said all those dreadful things about her? How arrogant, how unfair; he didn't even know her! And surely Fiesta could have spoken up for her more loyally? She'd done her very best for Josh and Fiesta knew it, so why hadn't she told him more forcefully?

Her pulse rate levelled and common sense prevailed at last as she kicked surf at the water's edge. But perhaps Fiesta was even now telling that poor excuse for a father just how good for Josh she was when he should have been doing the job himself! But she had to concede that Daniel Kennedy had sounded, if in a brutal way, caring as to who was looking after his son. At the expense of her emotions and senses, though, Karis thought miserably. Why make excuses for him? He was the father from hell!

'And while you are out here gazing at the stars who the devil is watching over my son?'

Karis's heart missed several beats as her elbow was imprisoned in a vice-like grip and she was hauled back from the surf and onto dry sand. She was whirled around to face her accuser, judge and jury! Condemned before she'd had a chance to speak in defence of herself!

Menacing clouds tore apart to reveal the moon and his stern features were clearly visible as he held her firmly, his eyes steely and accusing. Daniel Kennedy.

Recovering quickly, Karis lifted her chin defiantly and shook her arm from his grasp, and when she spoke her voice was clear and controlled because his insults had angered her so much it had fired her adrenalin, spicing up her strength, giving her courage to stand up for herself.

'Your son is in good hands,' she told him confidently. 'He is asleep and I'm not gazing at the stars as if I've nothing better to do. I don't default in my duties as your son's carer—

even if I am seen as wild and unkempt,' she added meaningfully.

He looked perplexed for a moment, not understanding the last statement. Karis put him out of his misery at the expense of her own. 'I came over to the plantation house to see Fiesta and overheard you both talking,' she explained. Her green eyes narrowed. 'I walked away when you hit the illegitimate bit,' she added thinly, and then, giving him a last look of indifference, turned and walked away again. He didn't follow.

She was still angry and hurt but managed to hide it as she dismissed Saffron, thanking her for staying on to watch over the sleeping children and promising her she would tell her everything in the morning. Saffron seemed satisfied with the promise of a gossip the next day and said nothing but a warm goodnight as she left.

Karis poured herself a fruit juice and took it onto the candlelit verandah to drink it and cool herself down after what she had heard from Daniel Kennedy—his angry implication that she wasn't doing her job properly. How that hurtful remark made her blood boil. That he should come here after goodness knew how long and start—

'I'd like to see my son.'

Like a spectre, he had suddenly appeared at the rail of the verandah. Karis looked at him with wide, surprised eyes. At least he had asked—or maybe she was misinterpreting his change of tone and that was an order, not a request.

'He's asleep,' she told him quietly.

He stepped up onto the verandah and Karis was able to see him better in the glow of the candles. He wore tropical whites and was an incredibly forbidding creature. Darkly good-looking and charismatic, with an air of mystery about him, he obviously had the capability of charming the birds from the trees, but not with Karis. As his unyielding eyes challenged hers frostily she was chilled through, in spite of the heat of the tropical night.

'I said I'd like to see him and I wasn't asking your permission,' he stated flatly.

Karis hesitantly stood up. She didn't like this man. She hadn't liked him before meeting him so nothing was new. He had a serious attitude problem. He had nothing good to say about her and that was unjustified because he didn't know her. But he was Josh's father and unfortunately that couldn't be questioned so she couldn't deny access to him, whatever the time of night. Without another word Karis lifted a candle in a jar from the table to light the way.

He followed her along the verandah and she felt his dark, disapproving eyes boring into the exposed skin of her back. Again those prickles of awareness played at the base of her spine.

Carefully Karis slid open the door and, holding the candle up, stepped back to let him pass through into the little boy's bedroom. To her utter surprise he took her elbow and urged her into the room ahead of him and then shocked her deeply by saying under his breath, 'I don't want him to awake and be afraid.'

With her heart twisting Karis stood beside him at the foot of Josh's bed. What an appalling admission that was. What dark past had these two shared? But at least by visiting him while he slept Daniel was showing some concern for his son's feelings.

Josh slept peacefully on his back, his head turned to one side, the sheet pushed down to his waist in the heat of the night. The child, in sleep, was unaware he was being gazed down on, Karis with love and caring in her eyes for she did indeed love the little boy...but the father? Karis dared take a sidelong glance at the man who gripped the brass footrail of his son's bed as fiercely as he had grasped the rail of the yacht he'd arrived on.

He didn't want to be here, she thought despondently. This was a duty call to his son. His face was set, unyielding, showing no emotion as he gazed down at the boy.

Then Josh stirred and in that instant Daniel Kennedy's lashes flickered. A tiny, fleeting reaction that had Karis's heart beating wildly in the hope that she might see some of the love this boy deserved from his father.

The flickering reaction to his son's movement was gone as swiftly as it had appeared. Stiffly he stepped back from the bed and so did Karis, and then the candle flame wavered as the movement of his body turning to face her stirred the still air around them.

'You have cared for him well,' he said, his voice so low and throaty, she scarcely caught the words.

A compliment? She hadn't expected one.

'To outward appearances,' he added, so meanly that Karis's heart nearly stopped with shock.

Once they were back outside on the verandah Karis slid the door shut behind them and lifted the candle so she could see his face more clearly.

'I don't think you will be disappointed, Mr Kennedy,' she said softly but firmly.

'I'd better not be,' he said thinly. 'I don't want to start my married life putting right all the added damage you might have done this past year.'

He gave her no space, no time to respond to that wicked, uncalled-for criticism. He was gone into the airless night before she'd fully taken in what he had said.

Karis stood for a long while on the verandah, staring out over the gardens and not seeing anything, trying to cool her anger and to grasp at the reality of what he had said. Starting married life? Daniel Kennedy was married to that beautiful but awful screeching woman and this was their honeymoon?

Was Daniel Kennedy divorced from Josh's mother and Simone the second wife or even the third or the fourth? Oh, it didn't bear thinking about. Poor little Josh. He didn't deserve that.

And it was none of her business, Karis told herself miserably and unconvincingly. The night seemed to oppress her and the cloying heat to press down on her and she was swamped with dreadful thoughts of that Simone taking over and being Josh's mother.

The pair of them had come to take Josh off the island. They were good-looking but seemed distinctly lacking in terms of character.

And then she felt again that mysterious snap of envy she had been whiplashed with earlier. She *did* envy that siren Simone. She envied her for being married to Josh's father and claiming Josh for her own and she envied them all starting a family life together because that was something she had been cheated out of in her own life. But that was all she envied Simone for; the rest of her feelings were taken up with pity. Being married to Daniel Kennedy must be like living with Satan's first cousin: hell on earth.

CHAPTER TWO

'HEAD tucked in. Beautiful. Bend your knees, Josh. Super. Go for it,' Karis encouraged warmly from the rocks below.

The boy didn't hesitate this time. From a higher rock he executed the most perfect dive into the warm, limpid waters of the creek. Karis raced into the water and swam strongly towards him.

'I did it! I did it!' Josh spluttered in excitement, his wet face flushed with pleasure as he bobbed up and down in the water, stretching his arms out to her.

'I knew you could,' Karis laughed as she hugged him tightly, and then tipped him back into the water and spun round so he could straddle her back. He screamed with laughter as she swam to the shore with him. Once they were on the beach she felt Josh stiffen suddenly. She let him go and he slithered down her back to the warm sand and stood rigid behind her.

Daniel Kennedy stood watching them from another outcrop of rocks, his eyes shaded by sunglasses, so that Karis couldn't gauge whether he looked pleased with his son's dive or not.

Josh had seen his father too, hence the stiffening of his slight body and his hiding behind her now. Karis moved aside because to screen him from his father was wrong, but before she could grasp his hand to reassure him he was gone, sprinting in the opposite direction to his father, back towards the cottage where Saffron was watching over baby Tara.

With a sigh Karis picked up her sarong to wrap around her wet, bikini-clad body while she tentatively watched Daniel coming towards her across the sand.

He stopped in front of her and stripped the glasses from his face. He was frowning and really Karis wasn't surprised. She doubted he smiled very much.

'Were you responsible for that performance?' he asked her tightly.

Karis knotted the sarong at her cleavage and tensed in surprise as Daniel Kennedy's eyes, frown and all, settled on the knot for a few dangerous seconds. For a newly-wed he certainly hadn't thrown off the cloak of bachelorhood yet, Karis thought ruefully. Obviously a man with an eye for women, which explained a lot. The second or third or fourth wife theory gained strength in her mind. Perhaps this Daniel Kennedy was into serial marriage.

Deliberately folding her arms across her front to hide the cleavage he found so fascinating, she lifted her chin and asked bluntly, 'The dive or him running away?'

The frown deepened and his concentration shifted to the defiance in her eyes. 'The dive,' he insisted quickly and quite challengingly, too, as if he thought her too smart by half even to have suggested otherwise.

Lucky for him, Karis thought. 'Yes, I've been teaching him. It was Josh's first perfect dive,' she told him, and then added, 'I'm Karis Piper by the way. We missed out on formalities last night.'

She forced a smile, trying to warm to him for Josh's sake. She'd given her own attitude a lot of thought overnight. She didn't like him and so long as there was an R in the month of April she doubted she ever would, but, putting personalities aside, she had to do her best for the boy and if being nice to his father helped she'd have a go at the very least. She even lifted her hand to him.

He took it and their exchange was brief but long enough for Karis to know he had blood running through his veins, not iced water as she might have anticipated. His touch had been surprisingly warm.

'Yes. I know who you are, Miss Piper.'

'Mrs, as it happens,' she asserted quickly, giving him a warning flash of her green eyes. 'My daughter, Tara, isn't illegitimate and I'm not a teenager either,' she added tightly, reminding him of what she had overheard last night. 'To classify me correctly you would have to file me under the emotion-weary widow heading. I thought you would have checked with Fiesta by now, seeing as you pay my wages for looking after your son.'

So much for the be-nice-to-Josh's-father resolve. But hardly her fault, she excused herself; he wasn't exactly the easiest subject to be nice to.

His steely eyes glared at her hard. 'You have a lot of spirit. I'm not sure that is enough qualification to be caring for my son.'

Karis's heart flipped in defence. This man was something else. Not real at all, as Fiesta had suggested when she had overheard them arguing the night before.

She met his cold glare with eyes equally determined not to be put down. 'I think being spirited is an ideal qualification to be looking after Josh, Mr Kennedy. *Lesser* spirited people than myself haven't achieved a smidgen of what I've done for him.'

'And what exactly have you done for him?'

His tone was unremittingly censorious and Karis gave up the struggle not to rile against it. 'Plenty,' she stated, and added with a sweet smile, 'Why don't you spend some time with him and find out?'

She stooped down to gather up Josh's towel and hoped her cheeks weren't flushed with anger. She really had tried but he was impossible.

'I intend to do just that,' he told her determinedly.

Karis straightened herself up and looked at him, her eyes

narrowed. 'Not before time,' she let slip before she could help herself.

He caught her arm as she turned away, a grip so jarring it cascaded droplets of water down from her hair to glisten on her sun-warmed bare shoulders. He let her go immediately after securing her attention.

'There is a reason for everything,' he told her quietly and seriously. 'Choices and decisions have had to be made for my son in the past, all with the best intentions and all unavoidable. Whether those harrowing decisions were right or wrong only time will tell. I care very deeply for Josh and I want what is best for him. I always have and I always will. Please remember that before you pre-form impressions in that pretty little head of yours. Don't fight me, because I need your help to smooth the path between me and my son before I take him away from here. Have I made myself clear?'

Karis stared blindly at him for a few seconds, wondering whether to argue with that in case he hadn't noticed she was a human being and didn't like being spoken to as if she were some newly acquired puppy needing to be house-trained. But she shouldn't care how he treated her because her feelings were immaterial; it was his son that mattered.

So, he wanted her to smooth the path for him, did he? The request was heart-wrenchingly sad coming from a father to a stranger who had cared for his son. And did he seriously think she would object to what he had in mind? That was even sadder. Couldn't he see how much she cared for the little boy?

'Will I have your full co-operation?' he urged when she made no attempt to answer him. There was only a slight softening of tone in the request.

Karis swept her wet hair from her brow to stop the drips of water from obscuring her view of him. 'I care for your son and care for his future too, Mr Kennedy,' she told him sincerely. 'I want what is best for him and if you think I won't give you my full co-operation then you are making a bad character judgement.'

His eyes darkened angrily for a fleeting second but then it was gone and he said coolly, 'Good. So long as you are on my side all should be well.'

On his side? What was this—a war? Well, if sides were to be taken she would always lean Josh's way. A child needed protecting. Josh was afraid of his father and there had to be good reason. Sure, she'd co-operate but Josh would always come first with her.

'When do you intend taking him?' Karis asked tentatively.

She wouldn't be able to bear it but she had known it had to happen at some time in the child's life. A year was too long to have cared for the boy, with no parental support. Every waking hour had been spent with him and Tara. She knew him as well as her own daughter.

'Sooner rather than later. Simone isn't fond of the Tropics.'

Had Karis just heard right? She stared at him in dismay. If this was cooperation she was out of it already. 'I don't think your wife is the first consideration here,' she managed to get out. 'I think—'

'Simone is not my wife yet and you are not employed to think further than the care of my son,' he retaliated quickly.

A mysterious surge of relief rushed at her at the news that Simone wasn't Josh's stepmother yet, not Daniel's wife either. But anger was in hot pursuit, bringing a flush of defensive words from her mouth for what he had just said.

'Just a minute, Mr Kennedy. That isn't fair. Yes, I'm employed to care for Josh and, as you must know, it hasn't been easy. You turn up here, out of the blue, expecting your son to run to you with open arms and then wanting to whisk him out of a settled life because your lady doesn't like the Tropics. What about Josh's feelings in all this?'

'That's enough!' he ordered thickly.

'Oh, no, it isn't nearly enough!' Karis went on determinedly. 'Child psychology obviously isn't your forte; as for being a father, you are even less qualified. None of this can be rushed. Josh's feelings must always come first. I might not have any official qualifications to look after children, Mr Kennedy, but I sure as hell know how to love them.'

In a fury she crumpled Josh's towel into her fist and stormed away from him, bare feet grinding so hard into the sand that they were hot and raw by the time she reached the gardens.

Regret for her outburst washed over her as soon as she stepped into the kitchen of the cottage to find a subdued Josh munching a biscuit at the kitchen table. She wanted to cover her face and wish it all away but couldn't because Josh would know something was wrong.

She hadn't any right to speak to Daniel Kennedy that way and she was deeply ashamed of her outburst now. After all, he was the boy's father and nothing in the world could change that. She shouldn't be fighting him, she thought remorsefully, she should be co-operating as he had suggested because little Josh's welfare and future were all that mattered. Trouble was, he made her so mad, stepping back into his son's life and expecting so much, so soon, and treating her with such disdain when he hadn't even given her a chance to show him how good she had been for his son.

She took a deep breath of new resolve. This little boy mattered, not her feelings. 'I've been talking to your father and he was thrilled with your dive, Josh. He said—'

A shadow darkened the doorway and Karis turned, expecting it to be Saffron with Tara, but it wasn't; it was the devil himself and on sight of him her skin prickled warily.

He spoke and this time he didn't shout or sound angry. He actually sounded quite pleasant. 'I said I wished Karis would teach me to dive too because I've never quite been able to do it. She said she wasn't sure so I thought I'd ask you. Do you think she should give me lessons, Josh?'

Josh stared hard at his biscuit, not able to raise his eyes to his father. Karis held her breath, watching the poor boy struggling with some sort of inner conflict he obviously couldn't cope with.

Karis glanced back at Daniel leaning in the doorway. Their eyes met and locked in mutual understanding and Karis was pleasantly surprised that his had softened considerably, as if he was sorry for being so sharp and censorious with her. He was trying; that was something at least. For Josh's sake of course she would meet him halfway, but only for Josh's sake.

She broke the eye contact first and went to the fridge for drinks for everyone. 'I've thought about it, Josh, and think it's a good idea. We could teach him together because you are so good at it now.' She laughed, trying to make fun of it all. 'But I bet he's rotten at it. Should be good for a laugh at least.'

Josh didn't think the idea at all amusing. To Karis's horror he flung the half-nibbled biscuit down and flew from the kitchen, out of the door opposite the one his father was leaning in. Karis closed her eyes in sufferance and said nothing till they heard the slam of a door on the other side of the cottage. His bedroom door, as Karis knew of old.

'You'll have to give him time,' she murmured, fully expecting Daniel to fling some sort of accusation at her for Josh's negative action. To her surprise he seemed to sag in defeat and sat down in the cane chair Josh had so rapidly vacated.

For a moment Karis felt a wave of sympathy for him. So far he had received one rejection after another from his son.

'A drink?' she offered, and started pouring juice from the fridge anyway when he didn't reply. She wasn't sure what to follow her query with. There was something so deep and emotional between these two that she wondered if they would ever come out of it father and son again.

'Is he always like this?' he asked at last. 'Still so sullen, unresponsive and hating the world?' He acknowledged the drink Karis put before him with a nod of his dark head.

Karis leaned on the fridge and sipped her drink, watching him from under her thick lashes. 'With everyone but me. He warms to Saffron too but not to the degree he trusts me,' she told him truthfully.

He looked up at her but Karis couldn't read his expression. It was beyond her. She almost wished she hadn't made the admission. If he had any feeling for Josh it must have hurt to hear that his son cared more for a stranger than himself, his own father.

'I'm sorry if that sounded as if I'm the only one that matters to him but the truth is I fear I am,' she told him. She let out a small sigh. 'He's difficult and it's been a battle. I nearly didn't stay when I first met him, but I think...' Her voice cracked as she thought about all the traumas she and Josh had faced together and overcome and what state the boy would be in now if she had rejected him from the off as all the others had done.

'Go on,' Daniel urged abruptly.

His tone said he *was* hurt and she went on quickly, 'I felt so sorry for him when I arrived. I had a child of my own and I wouldn't want Tara pushed from pillar to post and that's what has happened to him.'

His eyes narrowed painfully. 'Do you think I wouldn't have done it any other way if I thought it would have helped? I've paid for the best care for him,' Daniel responded flintily.

'I'm sure you have,' Karis relented wearily. But the best care in terms of wages paid wasn't nearly enough for Josh. She sighed and went to the table to sit across from him. 'Mr Kennedy, I don't know your circumstances and I don't want to pry. I don't know you and you don't know me. I understand how you feel, finding someone with no qualifications caring for your son, but Fiesta was right. Everyone else gave him up as a bad job and—'

'So why did you stay?'

'I've told you, my heart went out to him,' she admitted softly. 'I couldn't forsake him before giving him a chance. I suppose it made a difference that I was a mother and could relate to him. If that was my own daughter in those circumstances I would want someone to help her and not give up on her because she was so troubled. It did help being a mother myself.'

'And, from what Fiesta says, a mother with nowhere else to go and very eager for this job in paradise,' he said disparagingly.

Karis stiffened, her heart tightening at the truth of that. She remembered being evasive with Fiesta over her personal circumstances when she had applied for the job. Silly really, withholding her background when her very background was so important for the job. But she had been desperate to get away at the time and unable to think clearly and had just hoped that her eagerness to take on the care of the little boy would be enough for Fiesta.

It had as it happened but the fact that Fiesta had taken her on without delving too deeply into her past should have acted as a warning flare, and of course on meeting the irascible young boy she had understood why. Fiesta had been as desperate to sign her up as she had been to start a new life.

Karis shrugged away her hurt. 'That's true,' she conceded quietly. 'I was more than glad of the job for reasons that are my own but I'm not lying when I tell you I felt drawn to your son. Everyone else had forsaken him and—'

'And so you keep saying,' he interrupted wearily, and suddenly got to his feet. 'The world had rejected him and you were his saviour. What do you want—a damned medal?' he breathed, on the edge of anger now.

Shocked, Karis stared at him, her lips white. Why was this man being so cruel? Why was he always so angry?

Suddenly he let out a long sigh and raked his dark hair from his brow. 'I'm sorry,' he breathed roughly, impatient with himself more than her, she sensed. 'Of course you don't expect a medal. Look, this isn't going to be easy and I'm fully aware of the problems ahead. I want my son with me now. You have a special bond with him and...and...' His voice faltered slightly but he recovered quickly. 'I need your help,' he finished quietly.

Karis licked her dry lips at his plaintive request. It stabbed painfully at her emotions.

'Insulting me is going a funny way about enlisting my help, Mr Kennedy,' she said slowly and deliberately. 'I've done my very best for Josh and you're right, I don't want a medal; I don't even want your praise or your thanks. It's enough for me that he hugs me tightly when he says goodnight, it's enough that he trusts me. All I'm concerned about is Josh's future—the one you are preparing to offer him.'

Slowly Karis got up from the table and faced him. She really had nothing to lose by baring her thoughts and feelings to him. Very shortly her job here on the island would be over and done with. She dared not even think of her own circumstances when that day came because Josh filled her mind at the moment.

'I know I'm speaking out of turn here,' she started, 'and I apologise up front, but this needs to be said before we go any further. With your attitude I doubt if your son will have a very happy future. He needs care and attention and time and love and from what I've seen of you and your fiancée I doubt you could rustle up a fraction of any one of them.'

There, it was out, exactly how she felt about him and that awful Simone.

He was leaning back against the work surface, his arms

folded across his chest, and looking at her with eyes narrowed warningly. But Karis wasn't put off. She had more to say and concern and love for Josh made her brave enough to say it.

'All I've seen of you so far is a broody menace where I'm concerned, Mr Kennedy. I don't know why you attack me so when you have seen for yourself Josh is well cared for. I'm doing my best and I always have done and Josh has responded to my love and caring. If I didn't think the idea ridiculous I'd take it that you were....' Her voice suddenly went as if it had been switched off.

And then Karis knew. It swept over her, all-enveloping, all depressingly sad. She saw it all now—his attitude problem, his abrasive reaction towards her starting from the time he had stepped ashore and seen that she, a supposedly wild and unkempt teenager, held his son's love and trust in her hand. It must have torn through him like a serrated knife.

'Jealous,' he finished for her, in a tone that was dull and weighted.

Karis lowered her lashes. Her heart was thudding at his being brave enough to make such an admission. 'I'm sorry,' she murmured faintly. 'I didn't really understand at first and then, just now, I couldn't even say it because it's so awful.' She lifted her face and looked at him, her eyes wide and apologetic. 'You are jealous of me because Josh loves and trust me, aren't you?' she whispered.

'Yes,' he admitted. His hand came up and tore through his hair as if that admission had taken the strength out of him. 'In the short time I've seen you both I can see how you are together,' he went on roughly. 'Yes, I'm jealous of the hold you have over my son.'

Karis shook her head, realising that the snap of sympathy she had felt just now could be abruptly vaporised away by just one ill-chosen word. Did he mean to say the things he did? she wondered.

'Just a minute. The word is bond, not "hold", Mr Kennedy,' she corrected him firmly. 'I do not have a *hold* on your son. I do not like the menacing implication of that word.'

His eyes held hers stoically and he didn't retract the word or apologise for how Karis had taken it—as another insult. 'Hold or bond, whatever, it will pass when my son learns to love and respect *me*. It's what I'm here for after all. Then your services will no longer be needed and you will be out of his life and that is the way it should be.'

His sudden cool, calculated plans for Josh's future and her swift, cruel dismissal shook Karis to her very roots. She almost physically shrank away from him and in fact must have moved because his hand shot forward and grasped at her wrist as if he recognised she was about to tear out of the room before he was finished with her.

'That's the way it *must* be,' he said quietly, 'and you must have known that when you took the job on. Nothing is for ever. Now, if you have anything more to say on the subject of my son I would be pleased to hear it. Do you have anything more to say?' he asked, as if her life depended on her giving him a satisfactory answer. His eyes held a curious challenging glimmer.

Suddenly the firm grip on her wrist eased slightly as he waited for a response from her. Unwittingly she gave it as his thumb ran erotically over her pulse point, backwards and forwards, tiny strokes of fiery pressure that sent her blood whooshing through her veins. She felt sure he could feel it.

Karis stared at him in mute confusion. Why was he doing this—touching her so intimately? And why on earth should the blood rush in her veins this way?

Suddenly she couldn't bear the close contact a second longer and she snatched her hand away. He didn't protest. Her eyes flamed with indignation as she rubbed at her wrist but his eyes suddenly sparkled teasingly and it was such a sudden mood swing it shocked her.

'I'm glad you did that. I was beginning to think you were enjoying it,' he said smoothly.

Karis didn't need this sort of teasing banter to follow an intimate touch that had unsettled her so deeply. She lifted her chin because she wasn't going to take it.

'Did *you* enjoy it?' she asked directly, considering attack to be the best defence. He only smiled enigmatically, which was no answer either way. To her surprise she found her mouth suddenly had a will of its own. 'You did it so you must have wanted to. Your motivation puzzles me, though. Past experience has taught me that small, intimate gestures like those are usually connected with sounding the ground for further exploration but so far you have done little else but insult me so you can't possibly like me. So why did you do it? Heaven forbid it was a test of my morality.'

'Let me put your fluttering heart at peace, then,' he mocked, and Karis felt her temperature rise. 'Fluttering heart', of all things! 'I thought you were about to leave in a hurry and I wasn't finished with you. I realised I must have come across as a bitter father and I wanted to smooth it with you. Then I felt your pulse and it intrigued me because it raced so at my pressure. I wondered why.'

And because his eyes were loaded with mischief now she couldn't bear it. Her eyes narrowed warningly. 'Let me put *your* fluttering heart at peace, Mr Kennedy. My pulse races in *defence* of my feelings, not in *excitement* of them. I am your son's carer and just because I am on my own with two small children to look after that doesn't mean I suffer from a fluttering heart and the vapours when a man touches my wrist. In future we talk and think only of your son's welfare and future. I would like you to keep your lightness of touch and your suspect innuendoes to yourself. Now, you think on all that before you dare speak to me again!'

With that she turned her back on him and was down by the edge of the water on the beach before she had herself fully under control. The warm water lapped her ankles, cooling her feet deliciously.

His touch had nearly broken her. That small, intimate, tender caress, so completely unexpected, had very nearly broken her. She didn't even like him but it just went to show her state of mind when a stranger could make her pulse race so easily and effectively.

Karis crumbled to the sand in the shade of a dense palm and hugged her knees to her. Human contact, a man touching her, *him* touching her. No one had for so very long. She was always with the children, Tara and Josh, all day, every day, at all times. And when they slept she sat alone. Never anyone for her to turn to for comfort. No one to wrap his arms around her and just hold her. She ran a handful of sand through her fingers. Her life was just this, she thought ruefully: sand slipping away. No passion, nothing for her own lonely heart, just her life trickling away.

His touch, for whatever reason, had burned her loneliness into her soul like a branding iron. It felt like a searing, agonising scar on her senses and all because of a small, intimate caress of her wrist of all things. Imagine the effect of more, she thought desperately. The touch of his lips and...

She felt a light hand on her shoulder and she jumped in alarm, her heart thudding. Daniel was looking down at her and she felt her cheeks burn because of what she had just been imagining. He couldn't know but all the same she looked away from him and trickled more sand through her fingers.

He sat next to her under the palm. 'I'm sorry,' he said sincerely. 'Deeply sorry for hurting you the way I do. None of this is easy for me.' He shrugged slightly. 'You aren't at all what I expected. That first sight of you on the beach threw me completely when I arrived. You looked so young and natural, barefoot and with the breeze tossing your hair wildly around your shoulders, a baby on your hip and my son clinging to you for comfort. He was afraid of me and needing you and it tears at my heart for what I've lost.'

Karis drew painfully on her bottom lip as she stared out to sea. Yes, it must have cost him a lot of pride and pain to make such an admission. Already she had gathered that he was a proud man, a hard one too, a man with a past that had caused his son such misery, but here he was going partway to opening up his heart to her and making it right for his son.

'I need you to help me get to know my son,' he went on softly. 'I need your co-operation; what I don't need is you fighting me all the time. I'm partly to blame for that, I admit, and again I apologise, but meet me halfway, please. As you said we know nothing about each other and false impressions have been formed and that isn't a good thing. I *do* appreciate what you have done for the boy but I'm going to need more, much more from you.'

Oh, he might have apologised and he *had* sounded sincere but did that man have a heart beating within that impressive chest of his? He'd abandoned his son, after all, and now he was here to claim him back again and it wasn't going to be easy. Oh, no, not with his attitude and Josh's fear and her stuck in between the two of them, working towards losing the child she cared for so very deeply. Her emotions were flustered, to say the least, as she turned her head to look at him.

'Yes, I will help you,' she told him softly. 'I was never in any doubt that I would and you shouldn't have been either. If I argue with you it's because I know Josh and I have an opinion to air on his behalf. I want the best for him and I'll go along with anything you suggest—if I think it is right for Josh,' she added quickly.

He nodded and murmured, 'Good,' and they both sat for a while, staring out to sea, each with their own thoughts on what was best for the boy, though Karis's were punctuated with the awareness of Daniel sitting next to her. Such a strong, hard man, both charismatic and infuriatingly arrogant at times, and yet a small boy had the power to reduce him to a wreck of worry and concern. He cared for Josh, she now knew, and it was a relief.

'How do you mean to start this bonding with your son?' Karis asked at last, her voice low and concerned because perhaps he didn't realise just what a formidable task was ahead of him.

'I thought you might have some ideas on that.'

'I don't have the qualifications, remember?'

'Nor do I, remember?' he countered.

She turned and smiled at him and found he was already smiling at her. Karis wasn't surprised to find she did suffer from a fluttering heart but she was sensible enough to reason that it had come about because of more relief. It was better to be friends with him than enemies.

'We're going to get a long way fast, then, aren't we?' Karis said ruefully.

He grinned. 'Let me make a suggestion, then. Let's start by you bringing Josh over to the plantation house first thing in the mornings and—'

'Uh-uh,' Karis uttered negatively, shaking her head. 'First hurdle to be overcome. Josh doesn't go to the plantation house. I won't take him. If Fiesta wants anything she comes to us.'

He stared at her in disbelief. 'Why don't you take him to the house? I would have thought it was part of his life, mixing with people.'

'No one's ever sober there!' Karis protested. 'Is that what you really want for Josh? Association with a load of inebriate vacationers? No way. I won't allow that.' She got up from the sand and brushed her sarong down. 'If there is any bonding to be done between you it's not going to be done in that den of iniquity.'

He caught her arm before she swung away. He was frowning darkly. 'I thought you had agreed to co-operate?'

Karis stared up at him, wondering what the cause of his sudden about-turn in attitude was. She was only doing her best for the boy. 'Co-operating doesn't mean blind submission to your every whim,' Karis argued firmly. 'Of course I'll co-operate if I think it is in Josh's best interests. I don't think you entertaining Josh at the plantation house every day, surrounded by a lot of old soaks and languid, leggy blondes, is the right way to go about it.'

He let her go, lowered his head and raked a hand through his hair. Then he looked directly at her and nodded. 'OK, I agree,' he surprised her by saying. 'I wasn't thinking straight. I honestly hadn't seen it that way. So what suggestions have you got?' he asked.

Karis wasn't sure she wanted the ball in her court. It was his son after all. But she knew Josh better. He hated the plantation house. He was always much more comfortable at the cottage, which was his home of course.

'I presume you and...and Simone are staying in the main house?'

He nodded. 'Could you take one of the cottages in the grounds instead?' she suggested.

'They are all taken, and besides, Simone wouldn't—'

Karis looked at him when he stopped abruptly. 'Say no more,' she said lightly. 'Wouldn't have put you down as hen-pecked,' she added cheekily.

Because she was smiling he did too. 'Simone would delight in that remark,' was his only comment. Then he got back to the subject in hand. 'Yes, all the cottages are taken. What had you in mind?'

'I've left Josh sulking long enough. Let's talk about it on the way back,' she murmured as she turned to head back to the cottage. Daniel fell into step alongside her and as they strolled along the beach she said, 'Well, I was just thinking that it would be better if you and Simone were away from the vacationers, away from the main house. On your own, in a cottage maybe, it might be easier to handle Josh, but if they're all taken then—'

'I agree, but I hadn't planned on introducing Josh to Simone quite so soon,' he interrupted.

'Oh,' Karis murmured, surprised and relieved all at the same time. 'Yes, I think you're wise.' She turned her head and smiled, hoping to lesson the sting of the truth. 'It's going to be bad enough with just you.'

Daniel smiled ruefully without looking at her and nodded his good-humoured agreement.

'Josh feels more secure in his own environment,' she went on, feeling braver knowing that Daniel was warming to her suggestions. 'He has a routine that gives him confidence.' Daniel nodded again. 'I think it would upset him terribly to have that routine broken. I think we need a softly, softly approach. Firstly, of course, you must win his confidence, which is what all this is about really. I mean, the fact that you are taking him away won't matter in the end; when you have won his love he'll go off and...and...' Oh, God, her throat was drying up with emotion. Josh would go off with his father and forget she and Tara had ever existed in his life.

She cleared her throat. 'Yes, softly, softly. You should see him every day, at our cottage, not the house, and...and...and then when...well...when things are... Well, really what I think would be a...a good idea...'

Karis had stopped walking. She'd floundered to a stop as her words had dried and died. Daniel stopped too and turned to look at her oddly. He stepped closer and took her shoulders lightly.

'What are you trying to say, Karis?'

And she knew what she was struggling with. The idea she had for Josh's rehabilitation with his father was the only sensible course, but would Daniel Kennedy see it the way she did? He might take it all the wrong way, think she was being pushy and taking on too many decisions. But it was only for Josh's sake, and he would see that because he wanted the same as she did—Josh's happiness.

She took a deep breath and met his concerned gaze. 'I think that after a few days, when you have familiarised yourself with Josh's routine, it would be a...a good idea to move into the cottage with us.' There, it was out and it was the only way. 'You want your son's love and you want to give yours too and it's the only way you're going to get it together with him. Daily visits aren't going to be enough. Josh needs the whole commitment, everything. He wants to feel that in future you are always going to be there for him. Day and night and night and day,' she finished breathlessly.

Karis stood nervously waiting for his reaction, fiddling with the seam of her sarong at her side because another thought had suddenly struck her. Suppose he thought her suggestion was personal? After all that business with the pulse point of her wrist he might think he had turned her on!

Daniel stood studying the ripples in the sand at his feet, rubbing his chin thoughtfully. Eventually, after what seemed like an age to Karis, he looked up and nodded. But no smile accompanied the acknowledgement, just the nod.

'You agree, then,' Karis managed, adding deliberately, 'For Josh's sake.'

His eyes locked with hers and held them unremittingly. 'Yes, I agree,' he conceded at last. 'With reservations,' he added mysteriously. Then, with a very small frown of concern, he turned away. Thoughtfully, broodily, head bowed, he walked back towards the plantation house.

'What reservations?' Karis called out before he got very far.

He stopped and turned slowly and the look he gave her was darkly meaningful. 'If you don't know that, Karis, I shall wonder at your level of intelligence.'

He left her standing blushing to her roots, thinking she must be pretty dim-witted to have expected him to take her suggestion the way she'd meant it—for the good of Josh. He had taken it the way she'd feared. Oh, what an idiot she was. Reservations, eh? She could top his a thousandfold.

She marched off then, in the opposite direction, feet slipping in the hot sand and thrusting puffs of it behind her, symbolically kicking sand in his face because she was too distanced from him to do it for real.

'Josh!' she called out as she reached the gardens and saw him ahead of her. He stopped and turned and looked so pleased and relieved to see her, her heart tore for leaving him for so long.

'I didn't know where you were,' he cried, running to her and slipping his hand in hers. 'I came out of my bedroom and no one was there. I was all alone.'

'Oh, you poor darling,' Karis teased lightly, and reached across to ruffle his dark hair. He'd been in no danger. Nevertheless she felt a swish of guilt for spending time with Daniel when she should have been with Josh.

'I was talking to your father down on the beach. He's going to be around a lot, Josh, so I think we'd better be nice to him, don't you?'

Josh clutched ever tighter to her hand. 'Do...do you like him?' he asked hesitantly once they'd climbed the steps and flopped down to the wooden deck of the verandah. Josh didn't look her in the eye but traced a small brown finger through a dusting of sand on the floor.

Karis sat clutching her knees. Perhaps this was a time when she had to stretch honesty a bit. 'I like him very much, Josh. I like him because he's your daddy and because he has a lovely smile and is very good-looking—almost as good-looking as you,' she teased, and Josh looked up and grinned at her. 'He has been very sad living away from you and is still a bit sad because he worries about you. I want you all to be happy and a family again.'

The grin evaporated and tension bands tightened across the boy's forehead. Five years old and yet at times he had the wisdom of an adult. He doubted her reasoning. Oh, it was going to be a long haul.

'I'm happy with you and baby Tara,' the boy murmured, and Karis drew him into her arms. If she could have one wish now it would be that she could be in Simone's dainty little shoes, engaged to be married to the little boy's father.

'What are you laughing at?' Josh asked, turning his pinched little face to look at her.

How could she tell him that she was laughing because she thought she was going mad? Marriage to Daniel Kennedy wasn't an amusing thought at all.

'I was giggling to myself, trying to imagine your daddy diving into the creek. I don't think he'll be very good at it. Let's get him to try it soon. Now, this afternoon we'd better get on with some lessons.' She stood up and hauled him giggling to his feet and he tore off down the verandah to get his books.

Karis smiled after him. No arguments. Progress, but tomorrow was another day. Tomorrow could be a whole new ball game with this new life of bonding they were about to embark on with Daniel. And if all went well in another few days he would be moving in with them, as if they were a family.

Daniel Kennedy in residence. For her own sake Karis was already regretting the suggestion. Amongst other things it would be a painful reminder that even though she had a baby daughter of her own she had never experienced a real family life. Aiden, her husband, had cruelly snatched that dream from her. And Daniel doing the family business with Josh was just a practice run for the real thing. Marriage to Simone.

It didn't bear thinking about, Karis mused as she went along the verandah to join Josh, so she didn't give it another thought. Not for at least an hour.

CHAPTER THREE

'IS THIS the best you can do?' Daniel breathed, disappointed as he gazed around the small spare room.

Karis might have known he'd find fault with the accommodation and she understood. The past few days hadn't gone well at all. All the more disappointing because of Daniel's high expectations from the start. Karis had watched him rally time and time again after Josh's rejections and she marvelled at his patience and courage to go on. Daniel's daily visits had gone down like a lead brick with Josh and Karis had reasoned with Daniel that Josh wasn't stupid, he knew the visits would end with his father leaving him again, so was it any wonder the visits were so stressful?

The suggestion that Daniel move into the cottage sooner rather than later had come from Daniel himself and had been met with full approval from Karis—relief too. Rather he said it than her. She didn't want him harbouring reservations any more.

'I did consider giving you my room but decided against it,' she told him anxiously as he tested the mattress with the flat of his hand. 'I'm sure a double bed would suit you more than it suits me but Josh can't take too much of an upheaval yet. My room is next to his and—'

'OK, OK.' Daniel sighed, flinging a soft overnight bag on the bed that finally got his grudging approval. 'If this is all there is it will have to do.' Suddenly he turned to her and grinned sheepishly and his eyes indicated the pottery jug of hibiscus flowers she had put by his bedside to make him feel welcome. 'Nice touch, Karis, thank you.'

She smiled at him, happy that he had softened up lately. She fully understood the strain he was under.

'There's something else for you,' she said, 'pinned on the inside of the wardrobe door.' She nodded towards it.

Daniel opened the door and his grin widened as he saw the crude drawing stuck on the rosewood panelling with Sellotape. 'You're a better flower arranger than you are an artist,' he joked.

'I didn't do that!' she protested, laughing. 'Josh did. It was his contribution when he saw me gathering the flowers for you,' she added. 'He was too shy to display it on the wall, though, so that's why it's in the wardrobe.'

'What is it anyway?' Daniel asked, peering at it closely.

'Caves, abysses, ten-legged monsters. The lost world, I'd say.'

'All doom and gloom,' Daniel responded wearily.

Karis grinned and pointed to the picture, the tip of her finger stabbing at the only relief in the dark drawing—a round bright yellow sun in the mouth of the cave.

'The light at the end of the tunnel,' she told him.

'That must be me,' Daniel said proudly, grinning now.

'That's you!' Karis laughed, stabbing at the monster.

They were still laughing together when they heard a footstep on the verandah outside.

Simone stepped into the confined space of the room, forcing Karis to edge round a chair and nearly flatten herself against the wall. Daniel had given no indication that she was coming over to the cottage so her appearance was a surprise to Karis, not a pleasant one either. Simone didn't give off good vibes. Karis said a silent prayer of thanks that Saffron had taken the two children over to see her sister at the staff cottages. Simone would have to be drip-fed to Josh over a period of time. Moving Daniel in today was more than enough for the boy to take in.

'Daniel, darling, you can't possibly sleep here; it's far too poky. You'll suffocate. I've been looking around,' Simone went on in crisp disapproval, 'and this place is ridiculous. It's nothing more than a vacation cottage.'

Her dark blue eyes skimmed Karis from head to toe coldly and Karis realised this must be the first time Simone had seen her properly. She'd been far too fussed on her day of arrival to notice who had held Daniel's disapproval as they had come ashore.

Her frostly eyes turned back to Daniel, obviously satisfied with all she needed to know about Karis and coming up with the same opinion as Fiesta: she was the hired help, nothing more and nothing less.

'You can't possibly stay here,' Simone repeated quickly. 'Bring the boy over to the main house and get him used to the style he'll be living in in future.'

'Karis and I have already decided the environment at the house isn't good for him at the moment. By the way, Simone, this is Karis. Karis, Simone,' Daniel clipped, not looking at either of them as he unzipped his holdall and proceeded to unpack a few possessions onto the bed.

'Hello, Karis,' Simone offered briefly with a thin smile. She gave her full attention to her fiancé. 'Daniel, darling, did you hear me? You can't possibly stay here. This room is an insult...'

'Cue my exit,' Karis murmured to herself, and went to shuffle round the chair. Simone obviously didn't trade gushing introductions with lowly staff and Karis didn't want to hear any more put-downs on the living accommodation which was her home. And besides, it felt as if these two were about to have a domestic and she wasn't a part of it.

'Karis, could you arrange another pillow and—'

'Daniel!' wailed Simone in protest. 'You *can't* stay here.'

'Darling,' Daniel stated gently but firmly, 'I'm staying so

you had better get used to the idea. We talked about it and you agreed it was for the best so don't try and backtrack now. Why don't you run along and join the bridge party? You'll miss the first rubber if you don't hurry.'

Karis fled. She busied herself brewing coffee in the kitchen, the hum of the air-conditioning making it hard to concentrate on the thoughts that were swimming in her head. How could he be thinking of marrying that woman? How could Josh ever love her—how could he ever *like* her? How could *Daniel* love her?

'It's a bit small but it will do and with the door open onto the verandah it might not be too stuffy. Did you find a spare pillow?' he asked from the doorway. He was alone.

'I'll get you one from my bed in a minute.' She sighed. 'Look, I'm sorry about the room but it's all there is. My room is between Josh and Tara's bedrooms and they both need me if they wake in the night. The one I've given you at the end of the verandah is really only a store room; I cleared it out myself and...I suppose...well, I could move in with Tara and then you—'

'It's all right,' he interrupted in a conciliatory tone. 'It will be fine. I just didn't realise how small the cottage was at first and—'

'Perhaps you would all be better off at the plantation house,' Karis suggested quickly. Gosh, had she really said that? Forgetting all the partying that went on over there, the accommodation was certainly superior. It was air-conditioned throughout, with spacious, high-ceilinged rooms furnished with antiques, lavish en suite dressing and bathrooms, every luxury imaginable.

'I thought we'd agreed that wasn't a good idea.'

'We did,' Karis said quickly, 'but I'm not sure now.' She sighed. 'Simone opened my eyes. It's a very small vacation house and I'm sure she's right—it's not for you. She was obviously thinking of the superior accommodation over there and her objections to this place were well founded.'

'I don't think for a minute Simone's objections were fired by concern over the size of the accommodation. I'd be more inclined to think she was worried about us sleeping under the same roof in the heat of the tropical nights,' he said smoothly. He picked up the coffee-pot and poured two cups.

Stunned, Karis gaped at the back of his neck where his dark hair coiled into his nape. She studied the point intently rather than rake over what he had just implied.

With a very thin smile Daniel turned and held the cup and saucer out to her. Karis took it, shakily.

'Don't look so surprised, Karis. I did say I would move in here with reservations.'

'I...I thought they were your reservations, not Simone's. I mean, if this is going to cause trouble between you—'

'Josh is more important,' he cut in. 'If Simone sees you as a threat she'll have to work it out for herself.'

'That's a bit harsh,' Karis commented, though she woefully admitted he was right. Daniel had enough on his plate with his son without worrying about Simone's unfounded concerns. 'You think she does see me as a threat?' Karis added worriedly.

Daniel shrugged. 'You have what means more to me than anyone or anything. You have my son's love,' he reasoned.

'She...she doesn't know that,' Karis protested faintly. 'She's only just met me and hasn't seen me and Josh together and...and she knows nothing about me.'

'I've told her how well you have cared for him and how deeply he feels for you. And of course she has eyes in her head.'

'But she hasn't seen Josh and me together!'

He lowered one dark brow at her. 'That isn't what I meant. She has now seen you in person and...' He sighed and shook his head in mild disbelief. 'Don't look at me with such wide-eyed innocence, Karis. You know what I'm talking about. When did you last look in the mirror?'

'Gosh, I haven't got Josh's paints on the tip of my nose, have I?' She was about to fly to the mirror to see but the look in Daniel's eyes stopped her. Colour rushed to her throat and she lowered her lashes. She knew what he meant.

'Exactly,' Daniel said. 'You might have gone native while living here but you are nonetheless very beautiful and Simone has a pair of eyes in her head.'

Karis tentatively put her coffee-cup down on the work surface. She couldn't begin to accept that him thinking her beautiful was a compliment. A jealous fiancée on two counts—Josh and her looks—she didn't need.

'She has no reason to be jealous for either or both,' Karis told him firmly.

He eyed her curiously. 'I didn't say she was jealous, just feeling threatened.'

'Isn't it the same thing?'

He laughed. 'Oh, dear me, no, not yet. If Simone was jealous *now* your feet wouldn't touch the ground. But...' He paused and there was definite mischief in his eyes as he went on. 'She might get that way in time. But...' He paused yet again and Karis held her breath '...it's really up to you.'

Karis couldn't see the reasoning behind that. 'I don't know what you mean.'

He looked at her curiously again. 'You know, I do believe you don't. In spite of the fact you've been married you don't seem to have much grasp of what goes on between men and women.'

Karis's insides went very hot. Had she missed something here? Some tricky little innuendo he'd slipped in somewhere without her noticing it?

Suddenly he was very close to her—smiling too, which seemed more of a threat than his temper.

'It's really up to you how far Simone's feelings for you, or rather against you, develop,' he said quietly. 'And I'm not talking about how Josh feels about you.'

Oh, yes, now it was becoming clearer.

'Another *little* morality test for me?' she queried in a sweet voice but not feeling at all sweet inside. 'Like the *little* caress of my pulse point?'

'Morality test? Is that how it appears to you?' he teased.

'Well, yes. You said it is up to me, which puts the onus on me, and it sounds like a warning too: keep off or else suffer the wrath of Simone.'

'Hmm.' He smiled. 'It must have sounded like a bit of a warning.'

'Well, is it or not?' she pressed.

He looked maddeningly evasive, as if she had pushed him into a corner and the only way out was to disarm her with a touch of mystery.

He stepped back from her and took up a position leaning against the work surface across from her. Karis was suddenly aware of the slight whirring of the electric clock on the wall and briefly wondered if she was looking for distractions—anything but face this unnerving man with his mysterious suggestions.

'I suppose it is really,' he said quietly, holding her gaze as if trying to read her innermost thoughts. 'You see, the way to my heart is through my son, the boy you love so dearly. Simone doesn't know that yet. In time she might pick up on it; we'll see. But you, you are a sharp little lady. You already have the devotion of my son and that is halfway to my heart. Perhaps you'll take it into your head to go all the way. Perhaps that is what I'm trying to find out—if you are mercenary enough to use my son to win me.'

Eyes as wide as the coffee-saucer she had just put down, Karis stared at him in disbelief. Then she started to laugh because his rather bizarre suggestions could only be construed as a huge joke.

'This has all come about because I suggested you move into the cottage with us, hasn't it? You think I might be more interested in *you*. You think, because of the situation I'm in—a widow with a small daughter, obviously doing this job because I've hit hard times—that...that I'm a...a fortune hunter. And...and in with a chance because I'm so close to your son.'

She shook her head and couldn't stop spluttering. 'Daniel Kennedy, you are something else. If I ever came on to you, which I would never,' she emphasised strongly, thinking that was a contradiction in terms anyway, 'it would be for love and not for Josh or your fortune or anything. No, nothing but love and...and...'

She stopped because suddenly it wasn't even faintly amusing any more. Suddenly everything had gone topsy-turvy. Suddenly he was standing in front of her, close enough for her to feel the heat of his body. He tilted her chin up and kissed her very lightly on the lips and it was so quick it was over in the blink of an eye, which made her wonder if it had actually happened.

But it had. She knew for sure because her lips still tingled. And it wasn't fair that he should do such a thing. She stepped back from him. 'You shouldn't have done that,' she said in a small voice, but made up for the lack of strength behind the words by rubbing at her mouth as if she had tasted poison.

'I couldn't resist it.' He smiled down at her. 'It doesn't take much to arouse your indignation and it amuses me but I shouldn't wind you up so. The kiss was a sorry.'

So it was just a joke to him, a wind-up. She was a little temptation to be teased. 'Well, do resist it in future,' Karis stated determinedly. 'Because if you don't...'

'Ah, a threat?'

'No. Yes, actually, yes. A threat.' She squared her shoulders. 'I don't need complications in my life, thank you,' she said strongly. 'I don't need Simone causing trouble for me thinking I'm making some sort of play for you.' Her eyes narrowed, challenging him, her voice lowering to an accusing tone. 'And she would think that, wouldn't she? Because, after all, you are engaged to be married and I'm sure she wouldn't believe that *you* were making the advances.'

'So that's my warning, is it? Keep off or you'll tell my fiancée that I am coming on to you?' He laughed. 'How did we get this far, Karis? I believe it started with you inviting me to move in with you. An innocent enough request. For the sake of Josh, true, but already we have come up against a few problems. I think we both need to exercise a degree of caution, don't you? Hot, tropical nights and all that.'

Karis stared at him in stunned silence as he gave her a last enigmatic look with those damned enigmatic eyes of his and then strolled out of the door and along the verandah.

She couldn't believe him. All of that was down to him. She hadn't led him on, given him any reason to say such things and yet he had—said all sorts of weird and suggestive things. Oh, he was impossible and she was impossible for taking him seriously. He'd said he couldn't resist teasing her—something like that anyway. So to hell with him. She stacked the dirty coffee-cups in the sink and headed for Saffron's sister's cottage beyond the main house. Somehow children's company was far safer, and more enjoyable, than that of arrogant grown-ups who talked in riddles and innuendoes.

'I've taken the liberty of rearranging the hours Saffron spends here. I've cut them down in fact,' Daniel told her later.

Karis was on her knees on the verandah, tossing pieces of Duplo bricks into a box and generally winding down after the activities of the day with the children. They were in bed now and this was usually Karis's time. Time to cook herself a light supper and sit on the verandah and read by candlelight till she was exhausted enough for sleep. Those days were gone now that Daniel had moved in, she supposed.

She sat back on her haunches and looked up at him. He'd just sat down in one of the cane chairs, the squeak of the dry wicker alerting her to his presence. She hadn't seen him since the morning, when he had moved his things into the cottage. She'd gone about her usual routine with the children and this time she had been sure he hadn't been watching her as before. She had checked, looking over her shoulder so many times she thought she must be heading for some sort of persecution obsession. She'd come to the conclusion that he was spending his last hours of freedom with Simone.

'I wondered why I hadn't seen Saffron all afternoon. I had to make the children's supper myself,' she murmured absently, wondering what the loving couple had been doing all afternoon—swimming, snorkelling, making love?

'Did you mind?'

'Mind about what?' she snapped. She brushed the back of her hand across her hot brow, impatient with herself for snapping at him. 'Oh, cooking the supper?' she said more softly. 'No, not at all. I expected to when I took the job on. Saffron was an unexpected bonus when I arrived. I hadn't expected my own home help.' Thinking of it now, she supposed Saffron had been hired by Daniel and not Fiesta as she had always assumed.

She got up from the wooden deck, shoved the box inside and sat down across the cane table from him, wearily pushing the weight of her dark hair back from her forehead. Another few weeks and the rainy season would be upon the islands. Already the air was getting thicker and more humid, the nights were darker with cloud obscuring the moon. It would be a difficult time with movement restricted to the cottage because of the rains. With Daniel in residence it promised to be even more stressful; they would be tripping over each other.

'You're taking this surprisingly calmly,' Daniel commented.

She looked at him and smiled ruefully. 'What did you expect—hysterics? If I have objected to some of your ideas I've had good reason.' Though she wondered what reason he'd had to cut Saffron's hours. She was too hot and weary to ask.

He turned his eyes to gaze out over the verandah rail and thrummed his fingertips on the arm of his chair and Karis watched him. He was dressed in a dark green silk shirt and lighter green linen trousers, casually elegant but not casually elegant enough for dining at the main house tonight. It prompted a host of queries she hadn't clarified with him.

'When I suggested you moved in with us I didn't really give it much thought other than it was a good idea for Josh's sake. We haven't discussed—well, you know, domestic issues. I mean, do you want to eat here in the evenings when Josh is in bed or will you dine at the house with Simone and sort of come back later?'

He didn't seem to be in too much of a hurry to answer that one and it gave Karis time to think about the strain all this might put her under if he did expect to live with them as a family. She'd never experienced a proper family life herself. Her parents were professional people and home life had never been their top priority and her marriage to Aiden had been tragically cut short by his death. Now here she was about to venture forth into something she had no experience of—playing at happy families. It could be a minefield, with her past and Daniel's obviously shadowy past.

He smiled, not directly at her as he was gazing out beyond the verandah to the darkness of the gardens where fireflies hovered, sparkling like minuscule torches and then switching off as if they'd seen enough. Beyond, the gentle swish of the sea on the shore soothed the sound of the constant croak, croak of tree frogs.

'I think it's best I'm here constantly. You did say day and night and night and day. We should be able to re-create a true family atmosphere for Josh.'

So she was to act Simone's part for her, was she? He was back in the role of father and they were to play happy families till it was time for them to leave. Karis screwed her fists into balls. She wouldn't be able to bear the day of parting when it came. How could she go through this charade, preparing Josh for a new life with a father he hardly knew and didn't like very much and a new mother who Karis knew, just knew, Josh wouldn't like?

'I realise cutting Saffron's hours will mean more work for you but it will be better for Josh in the long run. Do you agree?'

Karis shrugged. 'He is your son. It's nothing to do with me.'

As soon as she had said that she thought it was a pretty dumb thing to say. She knew he would jump on it immediately and he did.

'It has everything to do with you!' he insisted. 'I've told you before,' he went on, 'I need your co-operation and I'm willing to help you as much as I'm able. I don't want Saffron cluttering the atmosphere here. She'll come in in the mornings to clean and that is as far as I want her duties to go.'

'Look, I'm not objecting to the extra work...' Karis sighed. 'But do you really think it's a good idea to cut her out this way? Saffron is part of Josh's life, part of all our lives. She's there for us all when we need her.'

He narrowed his eyes at her and Karis could guess what he was thinking—that she was being pushy again. 'I'm here from now on and before you make some sort of disparaging remark to that let me tell you that Saffron might have been a part of

Josh's life here but she certainly won't be in the future. She's expendable.'

And so am I, Karis thought in dismay. Her throat tightened painfully.

'You know this integration into my son's life needs to be made as simply as possible,' he continued. 'I won't introduce Simone till I think the time is right, and Saffron needs to be faded out. He needs a man around now, not a gaggle of women.'

'A gaggle of women'? Karis was stung by that. Just when she thought it was going to be all right he'd come out with a misogynistic remark like that. She got to her feet, too tired to argue. 'He needed a man around a long time ago,' she muttered under her breath.

Oh, heavens, she thought wearily, she hoped he hadn't heard that because she didn't want to prolong this conversation with an argument. She didn't know the circumstances of their past and why father and son were so deeply estranged. And he was in no hurry to tell her so it was as it always had been—nothing to do with her because she was expendable. First Saffron, then herself? It was only a matter of time.

'I...I'm going to my room,' she told him. 'I'm too tired to argue with you. I'll go along with you, Daniel. I'll try and meet your demands but don't expect miracles from any of us, especially not Josh. He's a small boy who needs loving care and remember that is where my heart lies—in his future happiness and well-being.'

She turned away, 'Goodnight.'

'Sit down,' he ordered thickly.

'No, Daniel, I won't,' she told him, pausing at the back of his chair. 'This is my time now. I'm your son's carer and—'

'And you answer to me because I'm Josh's father—'

'And pay my wages!' she finished for him. She leaned towards him. 'Yes, an employee, just like Saffron and as expendable as she is!'

His eyes glittered in the darkness. 'Yes, you are expendable, Karis,' he told her quietly. 'Is that why you argue with me, make inane remarks under your breath, attack me for something you know nothing about—because you know you have nothing to lose?'

Slowly he stood up; tall and forbidding, he towered over her. 'Sit down, Karis. I'm going inside to make us some supper. Sit there and reflect on this conversation and *your* attitude to me. When I come back I expect some answers from you. Why you dislike me so intensely to start with.'

In defeat Karis slumped back down into her chair, her head throbbing, the heat of the night making her skin clammy. Did she give the impression of disliking him? Perhaps so by arguing with him, but to her it seemed they were all justified comments. Perhaps it would be far more prudent to put up with his idiosyncrasies and do as he said. But he had asked for her help and when she tried he took umbrage. He was no ordinary man, that was for sure. He was sharp and appeared to have everything going for him but why had he abandoned Josh? Surely he ought to tell her because it was important if she was to help him?

'I don't dislike you,' she told him when he came back with a tray of food. 'I did at first because I had a preconceived idea about you because of the way you have treated your son in the past. You no doubt had your reasons but till you tell me what they are you can't expect me to fully understand. I appreciate you are doing your very best for Josh but sometimes you say things that really make me cross, like just now, saying Saffron is expendable when she has devoted so much time to your son and to me. And you said I was expendable too and that hurts.'

Oh, what was the point? He was right. They were all expendable.

'Point taken,' he said quietly, but offered nothing more as he unloaded the food from the tray to the table. Salad and seafood and a bottle of chilled white wine to go with it.

Karis had to admit that, for all her failings, Fiesta never skimped on food and wine. Karis had always been provided with the best at the cottage. She wondered again if it was all down to Daniel, if he insisted on the best for his son even if he couldn't give him spiritual support.

'Tell me about your husband,' he said unexpectedly.

Karis narrowed her eyes in surprise.

'Is it necessary for you to know anything about my private life?' she ventured as he uncorked the wine. He sat down and poured two glasses before speaking.

'I think it very necessary. We are going to be living together and I need to be able to excuse your behaviour and moods which are certainly going to ruffle an otherwise quiet life.'

Karis smiled thinly. 'Getting to know your son is not going to assure you a quiet life.'

He smiled softly. 'Don't try and evade the question I asked, Karis. Shall we forget Josh for a while and get to know each other a bit better? And don't ask for what reason again. I've just given you one.'

'To make allowances for my moods, you said. I wasn't aware I was moody.'

He made a funny sort of snort in his throat, so reminiscent of Josh. She had to try, she really did, for Josh. She sighed and sipped her wine and it was delicious and made her relax a little. OK, she'd meet him halfway. They would trade pasts for Josh's sake.

'He died six months before Tara was born,' she told him quietly, lowering her head and staring down at the green salad and assortment of shellfish he had dished up for her.

'I'm sorry,' he said softly and genuinely. 'It must have been a shock for you. Were you expecting it?'

Her head shot up. 'Hardly,' she blurted, and then realised he must think Aiden had died of some terminal illness they'd been able to prepare for. She muted her tone. 'It...it wasn't cancer or anything.'

'Accident?'

She nodded. She'd never talked about it before and it was hard to bring the right words to her lips to express herself.

'Go on.'

Karis picked at a prawn, pulled at the head and left it lying on the plate, her appetite waning. She reached for her wine-glass but Daniel's fingers on hers stopped her from lifting it to her lips. She glanced up at him in surprise.

'You don't need that, not yet. Go on.' His voice was calming and not at all accusing. He smiled encouragingly.

She drew her hand back and clasped both in her lap and took a shaky breath. 'He drowned in a sailing accident in the Mediterranean,' she told him, rushing the words out because she didn't want to linger on them.

Daniel waited for her to go on but Karis simply stared at him blindly.

'Is that it?' he asked at last.

Karis took another shaky breath. 'You asked about my husband and I've told you; isn't that enough?'

'Not nearly enough. You're reticent about it so there must be more. Death needs to be talked about. It's the only way to deal with it.'

'I've dealt with it,' she asserted tightly. 'It happened. It's history now.'

'Your flippancy gives you away, Karis. It's a cover-up for how you still feel about it—devastated. But you said you were an emotion-weary widow,' he persisted. 'And that suggests that you haven't dealt with it and fully come to terms with it yet. And correct me if I'm wrong but I get the impression that all was not well with the marriage before your husband's untimely death,' he added. 'Am I right?'

Karis stared at him. How very perceptive he was. She couldn't think of anything she had said that had hinted at it. She reached for her glass of wine and this time Daniel didn't stop her. She sipped at it. No, she didn't need it. She put it down and gave him a small smile. 'You're very knowing,' she whispered.

There was a long silence before Daniel spoke again, softly and sincerely. 'Yes, I recognise the symptoms. Did you love him very much?'

There was another yawning, reflective silence before Karis could reply to that. It was such a complex question. She didn't know if her love had qualified as very much or just a little. Aiden had been snatched from her so early in their marriage and the shock had thrown her into such a deep turmoil that even now she was finding it difficult to assess her feelings. She thought deeply about it before answering him.

'I did love him. Yes, I did,' she murmured at last. 'I wouldn't have contemplated marriage without love. I was happy most of the time, I think, but—well, something happened just before he died...and then the shock of that and all that followed...' She took a ragged breath. 'I'm sorry, this isn't making any sense, is it? I haven't talked about it before, you see.'

'Don't you think that was a mistake, then?' Daniel suggested softly.

Karis lowered her dark lashes and stared at the stem of her wineglass. 'There was never anyone to talk to,' she admitted weakly. She looked up then, straight into Daniel's eyes, which somehow had softened to a measure of understanding and sympathy. She tried to smile, a funny little sort of half-smile. 'Do you really want to hear any more?'

He nodded. 'Yes, I do.'

Karis took a deep breath but her voice wasn't very strong when she spoke. 'Aiden was drunk when he drowned. I should have been on that sailing holiday with him and his friends when it happened, but I wasn't, you see. They were having a party, anchored out at sea, and Aiden was drunk and fell overboard and no one noticed, not till it was too late. I should have been there but I wasn't,' she finished on a half-whisper.

Daniel suddenly kneaded his brow without looking at her and she knew what he was thinking, what everyone had thought at the time—that she should have been there and if she had it wouldn't have happened. She wanted to get up and leave the table because she couldn't bear the thought of a censorious comment coming from his lips. But she couldn't move. Her legs felt like lead under the table.

He spoke at last. He lifted his dark head and looked at her, held her limpid eyes and spoke softly.

'So you feel guilty for his death?'

'If it wasn't so serious I could almost laugh at that,' she told him on another half-smile, trying to sound brave.

'So there's more?' he suggested quietly, leaning across the table to top up her wineglass.

'Oceans more. Do you want to hear it?'

'Of course I do,' he told her, and she knew he wasn't just paying lip-service to her. She could tell by the look in his eyes that he was genuinely interested.

'As I said, I should have been on that holiday but the reason I wasn't was because I had just had my pregnancy confirmed.' Karis sighed heavily. 'I can still remember the feeling that warmed me through when my doctor told me. It's one of those enduring memories, never to be forgotten. I was so excited, so happy that we were going to have a baby. I couldn't wait to tell Aiden. I rushed home from the clinic and cooked a beautiful meal and rehearsed what I was going to say, and then...'

Karis sighed deeply again. 'Aiden came home and was bubbling over with excitement about a sailing trip we had been invited to join that weekend. He was full of it; there would be all these influential people on board, contacts he could draw on for business in the future.' She smiled ruefully. 'It rather took the wind out of my sails,' she tried to joke, and then suddenly her eyes filled with tears and she reached for her wine and shakily raised it to her lips.

'So you didn't tell him you were pregnant?' Daniel suggested pensively.

Karis swallowed hard. 'I did tell him,' she said in a small whisper. 'I suppose that was the start of it all—the doubts, the hurt, the uncertainty of all that previously I had been so certain of. I thought I had a good marriage, you see, but Aiden's reaction to my news shook me terribly. He was furious, so angry with me. He said it was too soon, that we should have waited and he wasn't ready to have a family yet, if ever.'

Karis shook her head in dismay. 'So many emotions that day—such joy when I knew I was pregnant and then such despair when I told Aiden and he wasn't overjoyed. I think that was the worst night of my life, knowing that my precious marriage wasn't as idyllic as I had thought. I must have been incredibly blind not to have seen my husband as he really was—selfish and ambitious. I'd always wanted children and it shook me to find out that he didn't share my views. Until that night I hadn't known; I'd just presumed that if two people in love married then children and a real family life followed. I was so naive, blindingly so.

'Anyway, Aiden went on that holiday with those supposed influential people. I didn't go because I couldn't face a sailing trip; my morning sickness had just started.' Karis lifted her chin bravely. 'That was another blow to my self-esteem—that Aiden could even consider leaving me on my own and going off like that, putting business before me. I was desolate and then...then Aiden drowned and, yes, I do feel guilt because if I had been there I might have prevented it and even after all that happened later I still feel sorry because for all his faults he didn't deserve to die so young.

'Perhaps we could have worked things out if he hadn't been snatched away from me; perhaps when it had sunk in Aiden would have been happy to have a family after all. I was cheated out of knowing, you see.'

'I do understand,' Daniel murmured sympathetically. 'And there is not much I can say to ease that hurt for you but you said something about all that followed. Was there a further sting in the tail of this tragedy?'

Karis nodded. 'Aiden was the only son of close friends of my parents, that's how we met. He was a dealer in the City. After his death it came out that he'd been involved in some dubious insider deals on the Stock Exchange, fraudulent deals. A lot of money went down, investments for people he had met through my parents and his. His parents were devastated by his death and on top of that they had to suffer the indignity of a financial scandal. He was the golden boy of their life and it hit them very badly.'

'My parents lost face with other friends who had lost money because I was Aiden's wife and was presumed to know all that my husband was up to and...well, they are professional people, both lawyers, and the scandal hit them badly as well. All in all it was a terrible mess and along the way my feelings and pain were disregarded.'

'But you were pregnant, Karis. Surely your parents were supportive? Surely they closed ranks?' he asked in disbelief.

Oh, yes, they closed ranks, Karis remembered sadly—closed ranks around Aiden's parents, their closest friends. It was why she had escaped, unable to cope with her parents' disloyalty and lack of support of her. It had been the loneliest and most miserable time of her life, losing her husband, facing a pregnancy alone, just being so terribly alone.

'My parents are professional people,' she repeated. 'We were never very close.' She tried to force a smile. 'You didn't really expect to hear all this, did you?'

He smiled in return. 'It explains a lot,' he murmured.

'Like what?' she braved to ask.

'Why you care so deeply for Josh for one thing.' He filled her wineglass again and Karis realised she had drunk rather a lot and it was why she had opened up to him. 'You can relate to him more than anyone else. He's you when you were a child. Did you have nannies?'

'Two. They were fine but not...not like the real thing. A mother and a father who really care. My parents were so distant from me.'

'Is that why you despise me so? Tarring me with the same brush because you think I cruelly abandoned Josh?'

'I...I don't despise you.'

'You do.'

She didn't; she had at first but no, not at this precise moment. She was getting to know him and she had seen the hurt in his eyes when Josh had turned his back on him and knew he had real feeling where at first she had thought none existed.

Karis stared at her full wineglass. Be careful, she warned herself. She'd already given too much of herself. If she drank any more she might find that she was...warming to him? He was a good listener and sounded caring but it didn't alter the fact that he *had* abandoned his own son equally cruelly as her parents had abandoned her when she had needed them most.

'So...' She rallied and raised her chin boldly and gave him a bit of a smile. 'Now you know the sort of person I am. Unsure of myself where personal relationships are concerned because I was blind to one man's real feelings. A devoted mother to my daughter, who will never know the father who wasn't over the moon at her impending birth. Penniless because my husband's fraudulent dealings left me with nothing and I've had to resort to looking after someone else's child to make a new life for myself. All in all I suppose you could call me an emotional mess,' she finished bravely.

He held her eyes as unflinchingly as hers held his. 'I think you do deserve a medal,' he said at last. 'But you'll have to earn it some more,' he added with a thin smile which was gone almost immediately. 'Incidentally I don't think you are an emotional mess at all. You are a very brave lady—strong too. You put me to shame.'

And then he was gone. Not physically but spiritually. He'd completely closed off from her, staring out beyond the verandah, a million miles away, in some dark and secret place where she wasn't welcome.

Karis felt a curious coldness close around her heart. She felt utterly cheated. She had opened up her heart to him and in return he had closed his to her and the most peculiar thing of all was that it hurt.

What was his secret? He wasn't going to tell her.

Karis sat for a few minutes, sipping the last of her wine and feeling more vulnerable and naked than ever. Her skin crawled with rejection because that was what he had done—rejected her.

'I really am going to bed now,' she said quietly and determinedly, but she decided her determination was pointless. He would let her go because she didn't even exist for him at the moment. She pushed back her chair and leaned forward to gather up the plates.

'Leave it,' he ordered darkly. 'I'll clear up later. You get your rest.'

He said it as if tomorrow she would need every ounce of energy to get through the day. As she padded along the verandah to check that Josh and Tara were sleeping peacefully she realised she probably would and it didn't have much to do with caring for two energetic young children. And that was an odd and disturbing thought to go to bed with.

CHAPTER FOUR

THERE was an unearthly silence when Karis awoke the next morning. Her first thought was that she had overslept and Daniel had got the children up and was dealing with them and would come down hard on her for not fulfilling her duties. Some nightmare.

'I'm paranoid,' she moaned after glancing at the bedside clock. It was so early the dawn wasn't even awake.

Daniel Kennedy, she mused as she lay back and stretched lazily. He'd occupied her thoughts last thing last night and was still hovering menacingly in her thoughts on wakening.

He had upset her world completely, stepping back into his son's life and disrupting everything. She wished she hadn't told him about Aiden and how naive she had been about love and marriage. She felt vulnerable now, exposed and even more alone because although she had opened her heart to him he hadn't opened his to her. And she had expected him to confide in her after he had listened to her so sympathetically and this morning she was still feeling cheated.

But perhaps it was too painful for him to talk about it and perhaps when he got to know her better, trusted her as deeply as his son trusted her, he would confide in her. She wanted that to happen, for him to trust her and be open with her and...

Karis twisted her face into the pillow. Why couldn't she get him out of her head? Why wasn't she lying here and planning the children's day as she always did? Why was she worrying about him and his son and why did her stomach muscles tighten at the thought of him marrying Simone. Because she wasn't the maternal type and certainly didn't have the depth of feeling to be taking on the boy in their proposed new life together. Couldn't he see that? Or perhaps the fault lay with her and she was the blind one. Perhaps Simone wasn't the cold and unfeeling person she appeared to be at all and they adored each other, and perhaps Josh would come out of all this a happy, stable little boy with a full set of parents.

What was Karis's judgement worth anyway? She hardly had an unblemished track record of good judgement where love was concerned.

'And why am I giving myself angst thinking about all this?' Karis asked herself aloud.

'Who are you talking to?' Josh asked as he leapt onto her bed and kicked at the sheet to slide down next to her. Karis hadn't even heard him creeping into her bedroom, but then sometimes she didn't. She often woke to find him sleeping peacefully next to her.

'Myself,' Karis told him. 'It's what mad grown-ups do sometimes. It'll come to you one day. You're up early. Couldn't you sleep?' She tucked her arm around him and cuddled him to her even though the early morning temperature was already in the thirties.

'I heard noises.'

'What sort of noises?'

'Water running and shushing.'

'Ah, the shower. It must be your father. He's an early riser. I told you he was moving in with us.'

As always she had been honest with him. She had told him yesterday while they were playing with Tara on the beach. She'd rather he knew in advance than be shocked and even frightened by his father's sudden presence in the cottage first thing in the morning. Instinct had guided the decision. Whether it was the right one she didn't know. But Josh had made no comment yesterday, perhaps choosing to ignore it rather than face it. Now he didn't seem too perturbed by it. He was dozing off beside her.

'Does Josh always slip into bed with you in the mornings?' Daniel asked some time later as Karis walked into the kitchen with a beaming Tara in her arms. Josh was still asleep and Karis had left him to bath and dress her daughter before breakfast.

Karis settled Tara into her high chair before answering. 'Not always. How did you know?' She hoped he hadn't been spying.

'The walls are thin and I heard you talking.'

Daniel was making coffee and Karis moved around him, preparing Tara's cereal. It felt strange having him here first thing in the morning, as if they were a family. Karis tried to imagine Aiden in his place and then immediately deleted the vision. Aiden didn't fit and she felt a stab of sadness for something that hadn't been but should have been.

'The habit must be discouraged,' he said shortly.

'I didn't exactly encourage it in the first place,' Karis told him, flinging the fridge door open for milk. So here we go, she thought despondently. He was here now, taking over, and everything was going to be wrong. She wouldn't be able to do anything right by him. All that stuff about wanting to know about her to understand her moods was totally irrelevant.

'So why did you allow it?'

She paused from pouring milk onto Tara's cereal and looked at him stonily, not believing he didn't know why. Hadn't he ever had a life with the boy?

'It's what young children do,' she told him, giving her attention back to pouring milk. 'I expect Tara will do it too when she's big enough to climb out of her cot. It's security, I suppose. Josh wakes up in the morning alone and needs to feel someone is there for him. It's nice to have a cuddle in the morning.' She looked at him quickly, feeling she might be rubbing it in with talk of cuddles. 'In some cultures children always share their parents' bed,' she added quickly in case he was brooding over what she had said.

'Must play hell with the parents' love life,' he muttered, picking up a spoon Tara had flung from her chair.

Karis watched Daniel rinse the spoon under the tap and dry it before giving it back to her. It was a small thing, a simple hygiene measure that came instinctively with parenthood, but it affected Karis deeply and saddened her. Once this man had had a life with his son. Once they had been a family—him and Josh and Josh's mother. Now Josh was a lonely and disturbed little boy, and Daniel was bound up in some dark, shadowy past that he didn't want to talk about, and there wasn't a mother any more.

Tara, in her baby innocence, giggled at Daniel as she grasped at the spoon, her face going quite pink. Karis felt a thud of her heart at her daughter's reaction. At sixteen months she couldn't be aware of him as a gorgeous-looking man with charisma up to his armpits and be flirting with him, surely?

Daniel looked up and caught Karis's wide-eyed stare and misinterpreted it. 'I'm sorry. I suppose that was a bit of a tactless remark under the circumstances.'

Karis looked at him blankly.

'Must play havoc with the parents' love life,' he reminded her.

Karis gave herself a mental shake and a physical shrug of her shoulders. 'After my confessions last night I suppose you thought I would be offended. I took it for what it was—a joke. A year ago I wouldn't have done, though. I'd have probably burst into tears. I'm gradually shedding my emotional baggage so you don't have to treat me any differently now that you know all about me. You would be patronising me if you did.'

'And there endeth the first lesson,' Daniel teased as he

poured coffee for them both. Karis afforded him a small smile as she spooned cereal into her daughter's mouth.

'Did it upset you hearing Josh in my bedroom?' she asked. He must have felt hurt that the boy turned to her for comfort in the morning and it was best that he talk it through.

'I would rather it was me in your bedroom,' he murmured under his breath, and held her eyes long enough for her to get the message that it was another joke.

Heat invaded her skin all the same, though. 'In your dreams,' she teased back, and then decided the comment warranted more serious remonstration. 'Actually that was rather a crass remark to make considering the seriousness of what you are trying to do here—ingratiate yourself into your son's affections.'

He laughed. 'Is married life always so serious? If we were man and wife wouldn't we be allowed some light-hearted relief now and then?'

She gave Tara her cup of milk and cleared away her cereal bowl. Then she sat down at the table, dabbing at the dribbles of milk on a beaming Tara's chin, anything rather than dwell too long on that thought.

'But we aren't married,' she told him matter-of-factly. 'You are about to be married to Simone and you love her so you shouldn't be making flirty, suggestive remarks to your son's carer.'

'What's love got to do with it?' he muttered as he brought coffee-cups to the kitchen table and sat down across from her.

'What are you trying to say?' Karis asked warily. She didn't know how to take that. Perhaps he meant that even though he was in love he could still flirt elsewhere. Or that love had nothing to do with marriage.

He smiled thinly. 'What is love exactly? Do you know? With your history do you know anything about love and how it should be? Everything you told me last night leads me to believe that you are as much in the dark about it all as I am.'

Karis's green eyes widened. That wasn't any sort of answer and was all the more disturbing for its lack of clarity. Numbly she reached for the sugar.

'Only because of the tragedy that happened which caused me to backtrack on my feelings and try to work them out. If I fell in love again I think I would be more sure,' she told him.

'Only think?'

Karis smiled and stirred her coffee, studying the swirling cream. 'No, not think, I would definitely be sure. I've learnt a lot since Aiden died, self-taught too.' She lifted her cup and cradled it in both hands and studied him over the rim. 'So if you know nothing about love how do you know you want to marry Simone?'

Karis purposely didn't mention Josh's mother. She sensed that the kitchen setting with packets of cereal and coffee-cups around wasn't the right scenario for revealing his tragedy, of which she was sure there must be one. 'Are...are you marrying Simone for Josh?' she asked suddenly, the thought just coming to her. Although she had asked outright she was not trivialising the subject. It was serious and awful if it was true.

'The only thing I'm one hundred per cent sure of is that I love my son and want him back in my life and I will go to any lengths to achieve that burning ambition. I've been through hell and back and so has he and the time is right for giving him back his stability. My son needs a home. He needs a mother again. He needs me to give him all I've failed to give him so far in his short life.'

Karis swallowed hard and sipped at her coffee. She felt quite shaky inside. He would do anything to make his son happy, anything, even at the expense of his own happiness because happiness wasn't bubbling out of him now when he was talking of marrying Simone. He didn't love her. Or perhaps he did and was sparing her, Karis's, feelings because of what she had told him last night. She wanted to know, though.

'Not that way,' she told him, shaking her head. 'You just admitted you don't know where you are with love and if you aren't sure you shouldn't commit yourself to marriage. Love should be positive and—'

'Should be but isn't always,' he interjected. 'You know that yourself. Last night when we were talking you hesitated; you had to work out that because you had married Aiden you must have loved him. That didn't come across as very positive.'

She shook her head again, tumbling her hair around her face. 'That's different. I suppose at the time I knew for sure but what happened to our marriage made me doubt everything afterwards. I wouldn't have those doubts again because I've learned from them.' She finished her coffee and put the cup down and looked at him earnestly.

'Daniel, you haven't told me about Josh's mother and I don't want to hear, not yet, but I know it must be something awful and that you have been through a bad time too. You must have learned something from those bad times. If you don't love Simone you shouldn't marry her.'

He was watching her intently now, listening as well, and Karis felt confident enough to go on. 'I'm an outsider looking in and what I see is you willing to marry someone for the sake of your son. It *wouldn't* be right for him, it wouldn't be right for you and...and as for Simone...' She met his eyes, almost pleading with him. 'It isn't fair to Simone,' she finished lamely.

A dark brow rose. 'And how would you know it wouldn't be fair to Simone?'

Oh, this was getting too deep for her. Not once had he said he had any feelings for Simone, but she was a woman and she must love him. Was she hoping that in time he might learn to love her? Or was it something more mercenary? Was she marrying him for security, for wealth? She knew nothing, of course; this was just more conjecture on her part.

'I...I don't understand you at all,' she admitted with a small shrug.

'You don't understand that I want the best for my son?'

He held her eyes but Karis looked away. She got up to release Tara from her chair and put her down to the tiled floor of the kitchen.

'You won't be giving him the best,' she retorted. 'It'll be second best and he doesn't deserve that.' She turned and glared at him. 'He needs it all, Daniel, no half measures. He needs you, his father, he needs a mother that he can love and if you don't love her what chance has he got? Don't you know anything about your son? Don't you know anything about love and marriage and children and family life?'

His eyes darkened and slowly he stood up. 'I know about as much as you do,' he grated darkly. 'Don't lecture to me about something you have failed so dismally in yourself.'

Oh, the pain of that. It was like a stab wound into her very soul. Fury welled inside her and she wanted to hurt him back but with what? She drew in a breath. 'You bas—'

There was a dull thud and then a wail from Tara as she tumbled against a chair, bumping her head. Daniel was the first to reach her, sweeping her up from the floor and into his arms.

'Sweetheart, gymnastics at your tender age!' He smoothed her head and jiggled her in his arms and soon Tara was laughing.

Karis watched, her fury with him forgotten, concern for her daughter sweeping it aside. She had expected Tara to scream for her but she hadn't. She was quite happy to be comforted by Daniel. Total acceptance from Tara, Karis thought ruefully as her daughter clung happily to his neck, another confirmation that ignorance was bliss at times. The more she got to know Daniel Kennedy herself, the more complex she found him. There were times she could hug him because of his enormous patience with his son and then times she could easily thump him for something he'd said to her. Did he mean to be hurtful or was he so wrapped up in his own stress he didn't think before speaking?

There was a sound from the doorway onto the verandah and Karis turned to see Josh watching the whole spectacle. Karis clenched her fists nervously, her heart thudding helplessly. What on earth would Josh's reaction be to seeing his father nursing Tara?

'Tara's just had a fall,' Daniel told his son. 'She's fine, though—bounced like a rubber ball.'

'She's always doing that,' Josh commented without interest. 'I'm hungry.'

'Feed me or else,' Karis joked, quick to get her reeling senses together for the sake of Josh.

'You or me?' Daniel asked, setting Tara down on the floor again where she happily toddled off to her toy box in the corner. He straightened up and looked at her, as if waiting for instructions.

Crumbs, was he taking this integration into his son's life seriously or what? New man he certainly wasn't but...

'Can you cook?' Karis asked, a slight twinkle brightening her eyes.

'I made the supper last night,' he reminded her.

'That was more of an assembly job,' she told him, grinning. 'OK, we'll give you a trial. Josh likes scrambled eggs. Not runny, though.'

'I want Karis to make my breakfast,' Josh put in firmly, and went to the fridge for eggs.

'That's right, Josh; cooking is women's work,' Daniel remarked but winked at Karis as he said it. He then excused himself, not giving a reason but Karis suspected it was to go over to the main house to see Simone.

And as Karis made Josh's breakfast she found she missed him, which was quite absurd since this was only the first morning. Then she pushed away the thought of Daniel rushing over to see the woman he was going to marry and of course whom he really loved, because all that talk this morning meant nothing. And she comforted herself with one very warm, pleasing thought: Josh hadn't stuttered once this morning.

It didn't last, though. Josh stuttered his way hesitantly through his reading lesson before lunch.

'Well done, Josh,' Daniel enthused. 'I'm truly amazed. I'm sure I couldn't read so well at your age.'

Karis's heart squeezed. The boy had done badly and yet Daniel was praising him to the hilt. He really was trying and it was very touching.

'I think that's enough for the day,' Daniel went on, stretching his golden arms above his head.

They were taking the lesson out on the verandah while Saffron clattered away in the background, going about her cleaning duties with more noise than usual, obviously showing her disapproval at her revised duty roster.

Karis smiled knowingly at her as she came for them with her broom, shoving it around the wicker chairs briskly, a not too subtle hint that they were all in her way. Karis gathered up Tara before she got swept away too.

'What do you want to do now?' Karis asked Daniel, shifting Tara to her hip.

'What do you usually do at this time of day?'

'Swim in the creek,' Josh interjected. Funny how he didn't stutter when he was in a demanding mood, Karis thought.

'Good idea. Why don't we take our lunch with us and—' Saffron let out a tut-tut which Daniel ignored '—explore the island on the way to the creek? I've never looked around it properly. Will we need transport?'

'With the children, yes,' Karis told him. 'It's too hot—'

'Leave Tara with me,' Saffron butted in. 'She's only a babe and—'

'Would you like to come with us, Saffron?' Daniel unexpectedly suggested.

Saffron's eyes widened and Karis's heart thudded. There was a tense silence as Saffron weighed up the suggestion. What was Daniel thinking of? First he had cut her hours so as to keep her out of the way and now he was suggesting she accompany them on an outing.

'No, sir. I don't think so,' she said at last. 'I don't like that old motor.' She paused to lean on her broom and then smiled such a big smile that Karis's heart rate returned to normal. 'You go without me. I'll get the food ready for you. Come on, Josh, you can help.' She propped up her broom and took Josh's hand and led him away.

'Thank you, Saffron,' Daniel called out to her. 'And do food for Tara; we'll take her with us. Josh will like that.'

'Yes, sir,' Saffron called, and though she didn't turn Karis knew she was smiling.

'What was that all about?' Karis asked, wide-eyed, when they had disappeared into the kitchen along the verandah. She didn't understand this man at times.

'Diplomacy,' he told her with a smile. 'I thought about what you said. Saffron is a part of Josh's life.'

'But not a part of his future,' she reminded him.

He nodded. 'True, but too many upheavals in his life too soon isn't such a good idea, as you rightly said. Softly, softly, eh? And, talking of softly, softly, I'm deeply sorry about that remark I made just before Tara had her fall. It was totally uncalled for and I regret it very much.'

Karis met and held his dark eyes, which were warmer than

she had ever seen them before. The remark had hurt and it must have shown for it had troubled him into an apology. She felt a peculiar stirring inside her. He was human, she was beginning to realise, and making an enormous effort for his son's sake, but was this feeling inside her all to do with his caring for Josh? It shouldn't be anything else but...

'Apology accepted,' she said brightly. 'I'll think of a way to get back at you so don't go all soft and complaisant on me. Some chance,' she added with a laugh. 'Right, we'd better get ready, then.'

'Yes, we had,' he said softly, still holding her eyes. He got up, breaking the eye contact that was making her feel very edgy. 'The motor. Is it that clapped-out old Mini Moke I've seen parked round the back?'

Karis nodded with a smile. 'I'm afraid so. Fiesta put it at my disposal when I arrived.'

'"Disposal" sounds an apt word for it. Do you use it often?'

'Hardly at all. The island really is very small. Everything we need is almost here on the doorstep. The creek is within fifteen minutes' amble and the beach is just there and there are the gardens of course.'

'What a tight little life you have led,' he teased.

Karis shrugged. 'It's paradise if you want it to be.'

'I'm sure it is,' he murmured, none too enthusiastically. 'I'll take a look at the dustbin on wheels while you get the things.' He turned away and Karis stood watching him as he walked down the verandah steps and went round the back of the house. In shorts and T-shirt he looked so different from when he had first arrived, all designer chic in silk and linen, with a face as long as a fiddle. He was devastatingly good-looking in whatever he wore, though, more gorgeous now because he appeared relaxed, although Karis knew that underneath he was still very deeply concerned for his son.

She let out a small sigh; for what she wasn't sure. 'He'll

have to shoo the chickens out of the Moke before we get going, sweetheart,' she murmured to Tara, and her daughter giggled and clung to her.

'Where will you be taking Josh to when the time comes?' Karis asked when they were sprawled on the white sands of a small cove on the other side of the island.

Saffron had packed two enormous sun umbrellas and Daniel had dug them deep into the sand. Tara slept under one, flat out in a cool, skimpy sundress, exhausted after Josh had splashed around with her in the warm, shallow water that lapped the isolated beach. They had eaten the picnic Saffron had prepared for them—small pastries and a box of salad and lots of fruit, mangoes in particular, which Josh loved.

Josh was further along the beach now, laying out a collection of shells he had gathered with the help of his father. Karis had watched them both, Josh quite stiff with tension, only occasionally speaking, stuttering again, Daniel quite stiff-shouldered too. Daniel had come back to the shade of the umbrellas, wisely realising that at times Josh was best left alone.

'I'm not sure yet,' Daniel said thoughtfully. He sat up and clutched his knees, staring out to sea. 'I've sold off my previous homes—a house on the Keys in Florida and a town house in New York.'

Karis gulped and twirled her index finger in the sugary sand. That sounded like serious money.

'When I take Josh back I'll have to make a decision about where to settle,' he went on. 'Wherever is best for him.'

'What about Simone?'

'Josh is my first consideration,' he said tightly, still gazing out to sea.

'Doesn't she have a voice?' Karis persisted. Poor Simone if she didn't.

'As I said, Josh comes first. If Simone doesn't go along with my decision...' He didn't finish, just let his words trail off.

'You won't marry her,' Karis finished for him.

He didn't answer but then she supposed he thought her pushy again. She had made it quite plain how she felt about him marrying Simone for Josh's sake.

'So what do you do?' she asked, realising how little she knew about him.

'For a living?'

'Yes, for a living,' she stated wearily. It was like trying to squeeze blood out of a stone. She wasn't asking anything unreasonable, after all, so why the reluctance to answer her queries? Was he afraid of giving too much of himself away? Losing his reserve, which was perhaps very important to him?

'Consultancy. Financial. I've built the business up so I can work from anywhere,' he volunteered after a long pause and then he turned to face her. 'Anything else you'd like to know?' His tone wasn't without sarcasm.

Karis sat up and coiled her arms around her knees. She was sitting slightly behind him so he had to turn to give her his full attention, when he wanted to.

'I'm not being nosy. I'm just interested to know what Josh's future holds. Where he'll be living, what sort of life he'll have when he leaves here.'

'Sure you're not wondering what sort of life I'll be living with Simone?'

'If I had anything to do with it you wouldn't have a life with Simone,' she said flintily, and went to get up but he swivelled and caught her ankle, making her flop back awkwardly in the sand. Suddenly he was almost on top of her, pinning her down with his body half across hers. She wore a bikini, he swimming shorts. It was inevitable that naked flesh struck naked flesh at some point.

The contact was electric, heat on heat. She tensed, her whole body tightening under his, her nerve-endings sparking like small flames of fire. His eyes glittered teasingly and as he parted his lips she thought he was going to kiss her. He didn't. He spoke, sort of gravelly, his breath warm on her face.

'And for what reason?'

She couldn't even think what she had said. The shock of him lying across her this intimate way was...shocking. Simone... If she had anything to do with it he wouldn't have a life with her.

'B-because of Josh,' she breathed quickly and heatedly. 'And because of Josh get off me before he sees us!' She struggled but he held her firmly, pinning her arms above her head as she lay sprawled beneath him. Her eyes were huge as she stared up at him, wondering what he was going to say or do next.

'Not even a little bit of reason for yourself?' he drawled suggestively.

Oh, this teasing suggestion was totally out of place and very much uncalled for. At times when she had his back against the wall with her curiosity he would come back with something like this, a tease, to wind her up and divert her.

'No, not for myself. I certainly don't care for myself,' she grated furiously. 'Why should I? What the hell have I got to do with your life?'

'At present quite a hell of a lot.'

'Oh, yes?'

'Oh, yes, sweetheart. Quite a lot. You have my son's heart and—'

'Yes, so you've already said!' she snapped heatedly. 'And I don't want to hear it again and—'

'Let me finish,' he insisted, his tone huskily low so it wouldn't carry along the beach to Josh. His eyes were grazing over her lips as if considering the risk of leaning down to claim them—well, at least Karis *thought* he was weighing up the dangers. And a damned danger it would be if he dared.

'Go on, finish, then,' she goaded, wriggling under him just to show she was still fighting him. 'I have your son's heart and...'

'And I'm beginning to feel my own heart responding,' he whispered, lowering his head to blow softly on the warm hollow at her throat.

Karis wriggled even more, her own breath tight in her throat, nearly choking her. 'Are you quite mad?' she spluttered indignantly. 'You haven't got a heart and if you feel some sort of response inside you it must be indigestion. Now let me go!'

He laughed. 'Not before I prove to you I have indeed got a heart and at this moment it's racing as wildly as yours.'

His mouth closed over hers, softening the tightness of it, softening her whole insides till she nearly melted. Soft and warm, hearts thudding together. Oh, God, it was awful, deliciously awful. She never wanted it to stop. Her whole body was on fire, little flames of delight and danger lapping at her senses. The kiss deepened and Karis inwardly fought the heady sensation of sinking down into a warm pit of sensuality. This shouldn't be happening, she thought. Daniel Kennedy, Josh's father, Simone's lover...doing this to her, kissing her so wantonly, wanting her so wantonly!

With a dramatic moan she tore her lips from his and with one enormous effort managed to wriggle out from under him. Of course he didn't want her. Whatever gave her that idea? In his world what had love got to do with anything? And that went for kisses too! After scrambling to her feet, hot, flustered, her ears ringing and her heart crashing, her next concerned thought was whether Josh had witnessed what had just happened. The boy had his back to them and was kneeling in the sand, scraping at a piece of driftwood with the sharp edge of a shell.

Satisfied and relieved, Karis swung round to face his father. He was propped on one elbow now, gazing at her with a small smile curving the corners of the lips that had just aroused hers so heatedly. The knowing look in his eye was what inflamed Karis now.

'I could kick sand in your face for that,' she breathed quickly, keeping her voice down. 'Have you no thought for anyone's feelings but your own?'

'You asked for it, Karis. I'm very quick on subliminal messages.'

'Huh! You have some fat ego. I gave you no such message, subliminal or otherwise. I didn't ask for it and you are very much mistaken in thinking that I might even have enjoyed it!'

'You did, though,' he teased softly. 'So did I, but then I already knew we would.'

'You know nothing, Daniel Kennedy. I did not enjoy it. I wouldn't allow myself to.'

'Because of Simone?' he quizzed quietly.

Karis felt the colour rushing to her face. Guilt. She should never have let it happen but he had caught her unawares and... There was no excuse but if she admitted Simone affected her so deeply it would be tantamount to admitting she did find him attractive and if Simone wasn't on the scene she would allow her feelings to show. And none of it was true anyway. *No, it wasn't!*

'No, it has nothing to do with Simone,' she bleated in defence.

'Oh, dear, that sounds dangerous, Karis. Have you no conscience?' he taunted.

Oh, she couldn't get it right with him. He'd twist everything to make her squirm and exonerate his own behaviour.

Karis placed her hands firmly on her hips and leaned down towards him, her body language way of saying she was on top.

'Has it occurred to that simpering arrogance of yours that I might not find you attractive enough to enjoy your kisses? No, I suppose it hasn't. As for conscience, you talk of mine? Where is yours where your fiancée is concerned?'

'Ah, we have a very loose arrangement,' he mocked lightly. 'Loose enough not to let consciences trouble us.'

Karis glowered down at him. She would never know if this was another of his teases. Well, she wasn't taking any chances anyway. 'It sounds as loose as your morals. Well, let me tell you something. I do have morals and I have a heart and I have feelings and they are not for your sport and pleasure. I'm a mother and a widow and your son's carer and I don't mess around with men that don't belong to me.'

'I've heard you don't mess around with *any* men.'

Karis's heart floundered and her pulse raced agitatedly. Fiesta? Oh, boy had she filled him in on her CV of life.

'No, I don't,' she whispered tremulously. 'I've had men come on to me since being here, inevitable with the rich egotists that come down here for their vacations. I don't go near the plantation house if I can help it but sometimes they stray, sometimes they ask me to walk on the moonlit shore with them, sometimes they come right out with it, no holds barred. But I take my job seriously and would never, no, never, expose my daughter and your son to what I see going on at Fiesta's gatherings.

'And another thing,' she muttered under her breath, trying desperately to disguise the hurt and anger that was welling up inside her. 'I take my heart seriously too. I can't afford any more emotional hassle in my life where relationships are concerned. I married a man I loved only to find his feelings didn't go so deep. I've suffered hurt and disillusionment and guilt over a man and I won't go looking for trouble so easily again.'

'Is that a vow of celibacy for life?'

He was still smiling that infuriatingly teasing smile. He was getting pleasure out of making her wriggle with embarrassment. And she was embarrassed, partly because the question had stumped her. She said nothing, just glared down at him as if the question was beneath her to answer.

Slowly he got up, brushing sand from his hands before firmly grasping her by the shoulders, quite serious now.

'There's nothing wrong with celibacy if you are lacking in hormones, but you, Karis, have hormones that need nourishing. I feel them thundering around your body whenever I come near you. You aren't being fair to yourself by denying them.'

Karis shook her head in disbelief and afforded him a very small, thin smile this time.

'Don't give me all that garbage. You insult yourself by saying a thing like that. I have feelings, Daniel Kennedy, and I want to protect them. I'm choosy too. You trying to emotionally push me into a corner certainly isn't going to influence my decision about you. You are off limits to my heart, because of Josh and because you are already spoken for.'

'And if I wasn't already spoken for?' he challenged lethally.

The question hit her where it hurt, right at the very core of her heart. It took her breath away. Her green eyes were wide and glazed as she stared up at him, her heart reacting to that pain, contracting sharply, almost a warning. She felt as if she had walked into a trap and iron bars had her in a grip she couldn't escape from.

'I...I...' She didn't know what to say. She bit her lip, forcing herself to come up with an answer. If he was free? Would things be different if he wasn't involved with Simone?

Her voice came at last, thin and unsure. 'It...it's a hypothetical question and—'

'Oh, no, Karis.' He laughed softly. 'Not good enough, I'm afraid. Your uncertainty is very revealing, though. I shall keep it in mind when next you try on the pious act with me.' His head swooped down to drop a small, teasing kiss on the tip of her nose and then he let go of her shoulders and strolled across the beach to his son.

Transfixed, Karis watched the back of him, broad shoulders, narrow hips, every muscle perfectly honed, an almost perfect specimen of manhood, except for one thing—that damned mind of his. It was tricky. He could expose her vulnerability with a composition of words that could floor her. She should have been more sharp-witted herself and not come up with such a feeble response to such a deadly serious question. Would he be off limits to her heart if he wasn't committed to Simone?

She watched him squat down beside his son, taking the piece of driftwood from Josh's hand and turning it over to examine it more closely. She heard Josh laugh and the sound cut right through to her heart. She knew in that moment that if Daniel Kennedy was free she might just *think* about allowing him into her heart and it was the most appalling thought that had ever crossed her mind. She barely knew him, and...and she was certainly no authority on relationships. But nevertheless...

'But he isn't free,' she murmured to herself. 'And a jolly good job too. One hurtful relationship was more than enough.'

And blindly she turned her back on him and his son and set about packing up the picnic things because enough was enough for one day.

CHAPTER FIVE

'WHERE'S Daniel?'

Karis spun round from Tara's cot where she was trying to settle her down for an afternoon nap. The child was teething and had been fractious all morning. Tara let out a wail at Simone's interruption. Karis gritted her own teeth and lifted Tara into her arms to soothe her.

'Outside somewhere,' Karis told her, rocking the child in her arms. Tara sobbed fretfully and clung to her.

Simone winced and muttered under her breath but loud enough for Karis to hear, 'How does he stand it? Outside where?' she added louder.

'Round the back, I think. Probably teaching Josh to drive by now,' Karis said with a laugh to try and ease the awkward atmosphere between them.

Simone swept away in a flurry of pale grey silk and Karis let out a sigh of relief. To give her her due, Simone was trying, if half-heartedly. She'd come over to the cottage every day this week. She'd given Daniel a few days on his own with them all and then she had started these daily visits, once with an expensive toy for Josh, a mechanical robot thing that made a lot of noise but did nothing to hold Josh's interest for more than the ten seconds it took to work itself to a standstill. She never stayed long. Karis always thought of her visits as duty calls, trying to show willing for Daniel's sake rather than Josh's.

At last Tara slid into an exhausted sleep and Karis laid her gently down in her cot. Karis stood watching her for a few minutes and reflected on the time spent with Daniel living in at the cottage. It had flown by but not without incident. Josh had thrown four serious tantrums and numerous little ones that had passed unnoticed by his father but not by Karis because she knew him better. Daniel hadn't thrown any tantrums but she had seen the strain build up on his face on more than one occasion and knew that he really had been on the edge of losing his temper at times. Twice with Josh when he really had been pushing his luck and once with Saffron when she had passed an opinion on Josh's eating habits.

'There's children starving in the world and that boy shouldn't be allowed to leave good food,' she had remonstrated at breakfast one morning.

Daniel had said nothing in front of his son but his disapproval of Saffron's interference had shown in the darkening of his eyes and the tightening of his jaw muscles. Later he and Karis had discussed children's eating habits. Karis was of the opinion that Josh's health wouldn't suffer if once in a while he didn't eat everything that was put in front of him; after all, adults could pick what they wanted to eat so why couldn't a child? Nourishment? Daniel had argued. Since when had a child voluntarily suffered starvation? Karis had argued back.

The discussion had ended on a note of hilarity when Josh had rushed into the kitchen demanding something to eat and Daniel had said if he had eaten all his breakfast he wouldn't be so hungry mid-morning and had reminded him that there were children in the world starving. Josh had then demanded to know what was so funny when Karis had burst out laughing.

So the time with Daniel living with them had had its ups and downs and Karis had been grateful for one thing: Daniel hadn't pressured her any more about hormones, giving her a chance to get those hormones sorted out once and for all. Daniel had exposed her vulnerability and her loneliness and though that exposure hurt at times she couldn't allow herself to dwell on it. He had stirred her emotions that day; it was no use denying it to herself because even now, hectic domestic days later, she could still feel the rush of excitement his lips had aroused. So she was starved of a man's affection but there were pleasures elsewhere to compensate... Oh, who was she kidding? That damned kiss kept her awake at nights and there was no compensation for that!

Sure that Tara was in a deep sleep, Karis left her and went outside. She stiffened when she heard Daniel and Simone arguing as they came round the side of the cottage.

'You're not being fair, Daniel. I want to go on this trip and you should be with me on it.'

'Fishing holds no interest for me, Simone.'

'Who cares about fishing?' Simone retorted. 'The Haslems will be on board and you know how influential they are. The Trainers too; you know his father is chairman of—'

'I know exactly who they are,' Daniel said in sufferance. 'And I'm not here to socialise or to pick up contacts. If you want to go you'll have to go alone.'

'To hell with you!' Simone exploded, and flounced off, gathering her flowing skirt around her legs as she pushed through the shrubbery in the direction of the plantation house where obviously all her aspirations lay.

What she had just overheard ground into Karis's memory banks. Simone and Aiden would have made the perfect couple, she thought ruefully, and then shivered and dredged up her sense of humour from somewhere.

'True love never runs smoothly,' Karis teased, sitting on the top step of the verandah as an angry Daniel strode past her. He stopped and glared down at her upturned face.

'And that is quite enough of that!' he rapped.

Karis shrugged. 'It wasn't said with malice. Just thought you might need cheering up.'

'And why should you think I need cheering up?' he grated.

'Forget it,' Karis breathed, and got to her bare feet to face him. 'Where's Josh?'

Daniel's shoulders slumped. 'He's gone over to Saffron's cottage. The boy bores easily. Just when I thought we'd hit a common interest.'

Karis smiled cheekily. 'Yes, well, I suppose a lesson in internal combustion is a little adventurous for a five-year-old.'

His mouth broke into a grin at last. 'You're right, of course, as you usually are.' He plunged his hands deep into the pockets of his shabby khaki Bermuda shorts, a garment of clothing Karis would have put money on that he hadn't possessed when he had arrived. He was always surprising her lately.

'How are the sore gums?' he added.

Surprised yet again, Karis raised her brows quizzically.

'Not yours,' he grinned. 'Tara's.'

He'd noticed Tara was teething—amazing for a man who hadn't a very strong hold on all things paternal.

'It's awful what babies and children have to put up with.' Karis smiled. 'I'm sure if adults were teething they'd kick up a worse din.'

'I doubt I could compete with Tara. She takes all the prizes for raising the roof at the dead of night.'

It had been a fretful night for her and the whole household, apparently. 'Did she keep you awake?' Karis asked worriedly.

Daniel simply shrugged and smiled as if it was all par for the course. It made Karis think about Simone's under-breath comment, 'How does he stand it?' He appeared to be standing it very well.

'Did...did you mind?'

'Losing sleep? No, of course not. I was more concerned for her suffering.'

Karis felt a sort of warm glow inside her. She was getting used to these warm glows lately, dangerous though they were. Daniel was turning out to be quite a caring man and sometimes

Karis felt it would be a lot safer for her emotions if he wasn't. But for Josh's sake of course it was a very good thing. The little boy's emotions mattered and hers didn't.

'She's sleeping now,' she told him. 'Are you going over to get Josh or shall I?'

'Saffron's bringing him back later. I thought we'd take advantage of some time to ourselves and take a swim.'

'We're beginning to sound like...' She stopped, leaving the half-finished sentence flapping in the warm tropical breeze.

'Go on.'

She didn't—couldn't. She felt her face flush with embarrassment.

'You were going to say we're beginning to sound like a married couple, weren't you?' Daniel suggested with a half-smile, as if it was funny.

His dark eyes held hers, lightened slightly with amusement. Karis took it that he considered the very idea a huge joke. Which it was, of course, if you didn't give it too much thought. Trouble was, Karis was giving it some thought because she was making comparisons with her own short-lived married life. She was comparing Daniel with Aiden, trying to slot the image of Aiden into this new existence and wondering if he would have been capable of making as much effort as Daniel to make things easier for them all. Not much chance, she conceded.

'I wasn't actually.' She smiled. 'I was going to say "parents" and stopped because it was a silly thing to say because of course we are parents. You the father of Josh, me the mother of Tara.'

He looked doubtful at her explanation, frowning slightly. Karis turned away.

'Hey, what about that swim?' he suggested.

Karis smiled sweetly at him from the verandah. 'If you want to go you'll have to go alone.' She sarcastically echoed his words to Simone and then could have bitten her tongue because he would think she'd been eavesdropping again. She added quickly, 'I'm a parent, remember. Tara is sleeping and I can't leave the cottage. Maternal duties come before...' She stopped. She had been about to say 'pleasure', as if it would be a pleasure to swim with him. Oh, she did talk her way into some tight corners with him at times.

He smiled knowingly. 'Shall I finish that one for you as well?' he teased.

Karis shrugged in defeat.

'Before pleasure,' he said meaningfully, somehow adding an enormous weight to the word.

Karis managed to get to the kitchen without succumbing to a denial because a denial would sound so very naive at this moment.

He didn't follow. She heard him laugh, though, and then the sound of him taking the verandah steps two at a time and then silence because sand under your feet was soundless. He'd be on his way to the plantation house to make his peace with Simone because he had nothing better to do. He'd agree to the beastly fishing trip Fiesta was organising on the yacht—one of those trips that took several days, with much quaffing of champagne and not a lot of serious fishing going on. And he would meet the Haslems and do what he had to do with Simone by his side...

And she would mind Daniel being away with Simone, Karis reluctantly admitted to herself. And swimming with him alone, a break from the children, would have been a pleasure she wasn't too happy to admit to either. In fact there were a lot of things she wasn't too eager to admit about her feelings for Daniel Kennedy, none of them making much sense. He was out of bounds and she knew it and just wished he'd remember it from time to time.

* * *

'Saffron made up a teething brew for Tara and it's worked wonders,' Karis told Daniel later.

Supper had passed and not without event. Josh had pushed a dish of pasta off the edge of the table, an action which Karis hadn't been sure wasn't an accident. Daniel had been adamant it was deliberate and had marched Josh off down the verandah to his bedroom, his son's feet hardly touching the ground. Ten minutes later Karis had crept down the wooden verandah, tiptoeing for silence, and heard Daniel reading him a story.

Now Daniel was sitting across from her at the cane table outside and staring out at the last remnants of a fiery and speedy sunset, lost in a world only he knew. He hadn't said a word since coming back from his son's bedroom.

'Coffee?' Karis murmured, and leaned forward to pour it.

'What was that?' he asked distantly.

'Coffee.'

'No, before. You said something about a brew for Tara.'

He was trying to make conversation and Karis recognised it and understood. He looked tired, as if Josh was wearing him ragged, which he was of course. She told him about the brew Saffron had made up for Tara and then immediately switched the conversation to Josh.

'He's testing you,' she began, pushing a cup of coffee towards him. 'Seeing how far he can push you. He wants your reaction. He wants you to discipline him; that proves that you love him because if you let him get away with it it means you don't really care. Don't be upset by it. See it as positive progress, not a retrograde step.'

Daniel stared at her in astonishment. 'How come you know so much and I don't?'

'You do,' she insisted. 'You do the right things but you don't really know why. Parenting is instinctive. It's why some are good at it and some aren't. Women are generally better at it than men because they are programmed that way. I'm sure a million feminists would be onto me like a ton of bricks if they heard that but you can't change the truth. Women are made that way.' She smiled at him encouragingly. 'You are doing very well and Josh is respecting you.'

'I don't want his respect. I want what he gives to you—his love.'

'You can't have one without the other.' She laughed.

There was a silence, as if Daniel was considering what she had said.

'Aiden was a fool,' he said unexpectedly.

Karis raised a brow in surprise.

'If you had been my wife I wouldn't have treated you so shabbily.' He looked past her, gone again, into that world of his where the past lurked, no doubt.

Karis was silent with him for a few minutes, pondering those words. They had been spoken with sincerity, as if he really would have cherished her as his wife. But he was simply musing, being kind to her—and grateful too. He'd have some weighty job on his hands trying to make it right with Josh on his own.

She took courage from his confidence in her and asked what she had wanted to know from the first time she had met his son. Now, of course, she was curious for another reason. She wanted to know more about him because she was getting to know Daniel Kennedy the man and not just the father. And it was time he opened up to her anyway. They were living together after all.

'What happened to Josh's mother?'

Silence. But Karis wasn't put off. Because of her own revelations about her past, and his sympathetic understanding, she persisted, understanding his reserve.

'Were you divorced?' she asked at last though she suspected not. Sometimes he was so far away in the mists of his past that she thought he should have come to terms with a divorce by now if that had been the case. But by suggesting divorce it would eliminate one reason and lead to the real reason for his and Josh's sadness.

He gave her his attention then, his eyes dark and unreadable but a small smile curved rather cynically at the corners of his mouth.

He shook his head. 'You don't want to know,' he breathed drily.

'I do or I wouldn't have asked,' she insisted softly. 'You owe me a confidence anyway and I wouldn't like you to leave with Josh as much of a mystery as you were when you arrived.'

'Sometimes mysteries are best left as mysteries.'

'Oh, very profound,' Karis teased, trying to lighten the atmosphere, which was getting a bit heavy.

'Would it matter if you never knew?'

It was a serious question and Karis treated it accordingly. 'Yes—yes, it would,' she admitted truthfully. 'I care about Josh and what is going to happen to him. You're going to take him away and it would help me to know why Josh has been so unhappy in his life. I could let him go understanding him better.'

'You might be so shocked it will put you off me.'

He smiled then, a real one.

'Are you really worried about what I think of you?' she said gently, quite surprised that her opinion of him was a consideration to him.

He didn't respond verbally, but his eyes hinted that possibly her opinion did matter. That was only her interpretation of the look, though, she thought, not necessarily the truth. 'I doubt you could shock me,' she added to fill the silence. 'My own past wasn't exactly without shocking incidents.'

'I could top your tale of woe any day,' he said ruefully.

He held her eyes for a very long time, a time in which Karis began to wish she had never asked. The candles on the wall flickered, somehow ominously, and Karis felt her skin prickle with a suggestion of dread. This was nothing to do with divorce.

'She...she's dead, isn't she?' she whispered at last.

Silence again. A silence of confirmation and Karis's own bruised heart went out to him. So, his wife had died and he was still in love with her and this was why he had rejected Josh—because he couldn't face life without her and Josh was ever a reminder...

'I'm sorry, truly sorry,' she murmured with sincerity.

And then, in the following silence, she let her imagination run riot. He must have loved her so deeply, almost to the point of obsession, because he obviously hadn't coped with her death. Karis felt a deep envy drag inside her for the wonderful marriage they must have had. Aiden hadn't really loved her to the depth she had hoped for in their brief marriage. He wouldn't have left her, pregnant and alone, while he went sailing the Med if he had. Yes, she envied Daniel's deceased wife; she envied the love he still had for her. He couldn't love Simone in the same way and yet he was willing to marry her to give Josh a stable family life at last. It was all a terrible tragedy but that obsessional love for his wife had damaged his son. Didn't Daniel realise that?

Karis leaned forward across the table. 'Daniel, please don't think I'm speaking out of turn,' she said softly. 'I understand how you must feel, how much you must still miss her, but...but think of Josh. I mean, that poor little boy needed you after his mother died. I know grief can cripple you but how could you have let that little boy go?'

'Do you think I would have allowed that to happen if I could have avoided it?' he said abruptly.

Karis shook her head. 'Of course not, but you were hurting and sometimes...sometimes love can twist your thinking and make you do and say things that should have had more consideration. You were mourning the death of your wife and—'

His hand came across the table-top and grasped at her wrist. 'Love didn't twist my thinking after she died,' he told her roughly. 'There, I've shocked you. Do you want to hear more?'

Dazed, Karis stared at him. So often he had hinted that he knew nothing about love, but he must have loved his wife, surely?

'Yes. Yes, I do want to hear more,' she said faintly.

'You don't sound very sure.'

'I...I want to understand, like...like you wanted to understand about me.'

He let go of her wrist and got up from the table, putting distance between them. He stood by the verandah rail, gripping it as he had gripped the rail of the yacht he'd arrived on. He seemed to have that same reluctance about him now, shoulders stiff and unyielding as if he didn't want to be here. Of course he didn't have to tell her anything but she had pushed him and perhaps he felt he owed it to her after all she had told him about her marriage to Aiden.

But if she was going to have to drag it out of him perhaps it was best left alone. She wanted to say that if he didn't want to tell her she would respect his wishes but she didn't get the chance.

'Guilt twisted my thinking after her death,' he admitted softly. 'I might have been able to prevent it, you see. But I wasn't there and I should have been. When you were telling me about what happened to your husband I knew just what you had been through. Every last aching, miserable, guilt-ridden emotion of it all.' He took a deep breath. 'Suzanne collapsed with a brain haemorrhage. If she had been hospitalised quickly enough she might have been saved. But I wasn't with her; I just wasn't there.'

Karis squeezed shut her eyes and her heart felt like lead with sorrow. So now she knew why he hadn't been as open with her the night she had bared her soul. It might have tipped them both over the edge if he had twinned his tale of tragedy and sorrow with hers. You could only take so much and that would have been too much. So now she knew and it explained such a lot.

'I was in Europe when it happened,' he went on. 'I was on yet another business trip, working, making money, for her, for Josh, or so I thought.'

Karis willed herself to get up and go to him. She wanted to be near him, to share it with him. She stood next to him, staring out to the same horizon he was looking at and hoping he would feel her silently reaching out to him.

'What do you mean, so you thought?' she asked tentatively, a small frown creasing her brow.

'I shouldn't have told you,' he murmured, his voice thick with concern for her now.

Karis turned her face to his and gave him a reassuring smile. She saw in his eyes the pain from the past and the concern for her in the present. 'I'm all right,' she assured him. 'I've been there, don't forget.' She sighed deeply. 'I'm sorry, Daniel, desperately sorry for your wife and all of you. Please go on. Is...is it hard to talk about it?' she pressed softly.

He smiled thinly. 'It's harder for the listener, deciding if I was guilty by default or not. You must understand that well enough. You see, after it happened I questioned myself deeply. It's inevitable you do after such a shocking tragedy. I should have been with her but I wasn't, I was away, driving myself hard, travelling, away from home more than I was there. The dreadful truth was that I was escaping.'

He shook his dark head with regret. 'It wasn't an easy marriage. There was love at first, of course, or so I thought, but it seemed I could never please her or give her quite enough.

Like you, I had ideals about love and marriage but they weren't realised. I thought Josh coming along would make her see that there was more to life than an accumulation of all things material.'

'Did it?' Karis whispered.

'She looked after him well enough—she would have lost face with her society friends if she hadn't—but I don't think her heart was ever in motherhood. She wanted a child but when Josh arrived he was more like an accessory to her lifestyle than a lifelong dedication. I adored the boy; right from the first moment I saw him I adored him, and that seemed to make matters worse for her. I sometimes thought she was jealous, perhaps feeling guilty that she couldn't feel the way I felt about Josh and resenting me for it. No matter how hard I tried she couldn't find contentment in her life and maybe that was my fault; maybe I failed her in some way.'

'No, Daniel, not your fault. People are made the way they are and sometimes nothing can change them,' Karis insisted. 'Marriage is a minefield,' she whispered beside him. 'We take it on not realising that sometimes love isn't enough.'

He turned to her then and leaned back against the wooden rail. His hand came up and pushed a strand of her hair behind her ear. 'And there was I thinking you were some teenager down on your luck and probably doing all the wrong things for my son. I've heard more sense and wisdom from you than anyone else in my life.'

She smiled. 'I don't know whether to take that as a compliment or not.'

'It's a compliment, I assure you.' He turned back to face the darkness again, as if drawing from its power. 'Suzanne died in our summer vacation house down on the Keys in Florida. She collapsed while getting ready for bed. The coroner said she had died at four in the morning. She had lain there all night. She wouldn't have known anything about it but if help had been at hand she might have been saved. The cleaning woman found her the next morning and...and Josh, crouched in his bedroom, screaming for his mummy.'

'Oh, no,' Karis breathed in despair, squeezing her eyes shut at the thought of all the little boy had been through. Oh, it explained so much. 'Oh, Daniel,' she groaned helplessly, biting her lower lip and fighting for the right words, but only an ineffectual 'How terrible' came from her mouth. There were no words, nothing you could say to ease that sort of pain for someone.

'He was sobbing in his bedroom, too young to understand what had happened, only that he couldn't wake his mummy.' Daniel sighed deeply. 'That was the very worst thing for me—the torment of wondering what he had been through, if he had woken and found her, heard her cry out or something, actually been with her when she had breathed her last breath.' His voice cracked and it was a while before he was composed enough to go on. 'The shock of Suzanne's death was bad enough, and then the terrible guilt that I should have been there, but my son...my darling son witnessing that night.' He shook his head. 'It was and still is an unbearable thought for me. It tortures me because I can't take that night away from him. He was there and I wasn't and a small, helpless little boy shouldn't have had to go through that shocking experience.

'Josh was immediately taken into care while the authorities tried to contact me,' Daniel went on. 'I'd just flown from London to Germany and by the time I was tracked down and flew back he had retreated into himself. He was little more than a baby. Two, nearly three and going through all that trauma. It was heartbreaking.'

Karis couldn't speak now for the grief that was tightening her own throat, and even if she could have what could she have said that wouldn't sound crass and ineffectual? Now she understood why Josh was the way he was, so terribly insecure and afraid. Now she could understand Daniel more and her heart tore for them both.

'Poor Suzanne and poor Josh,' Daniel went on after a long, reflective pause. 'Child psychologists had no effect. God only knows what was going on in his mind. I couldn't get near him. He shrank away from me every time I tried to gather him into my arms. I had to go through the formalities of the inquest and the funeral and it took for ever. In only a matter of months I lost so much business I was verging on ruin. All I could think of doing was getting Josh away from it all and trying to rebuild his life for him.'

'How did Fiesta get involved?' Karis asked at last, her voice barely a whisper. She lifted her head to look at him, her face pinched with grief for him. His face was gaunt, exhausted with the effort of reliving such a tragedy.

'She's a cousin of Suzanne's, the only relative. We were both only children, our parents deceased, and there were no close friends, only Suzanne's society friends, and God forbid I would put my son into their care. Fiesta came forward and offered to take Josh on. She said I would do better to get my life together before I lost everything and had nothing to offer for the boy's future. I didn't want to leave him but it seemed my presence made him worse, as if he too blamed me for the loss of his mother.

'I brought him down here to the island and went back to the States. I sold the two homes we owned because I didn't want to take Josh back to either of them. I wanted a new start for him. I built up the business again, security for Josh's future if anything happened to me. I had to do that; I had to leave him and get my business back on track. For him, for his future.'

Karis noticed his hands were gripping the verandah rail so tightly they were white. She wanted to cover them with her own small hands, to show that she understood and was with him all the way. But she didn't; she just stood next to him, waiting, because she knew there was more bottled up inside him.

'All for Josh,' he uttered at last, 'and perhaps the time was wasted because no amount of monetary security can buy back the love of your own child.'

'Josh does love you,' Karis reassured him. 'He just can't admit it yet. I don't know if you did the right thing,' she sighed. 'Only time will tell. If it's any consolation, if I was a man I think I would have done the same thing. Josh's trauma will pass because you love him so deeply.'

'I don't know how I could have made it any better for him,' he sighed. 'Fiesta bit off more than she could chew in taking him on but no one knew that at the time. The business has expanded for Fiesta since she started up and I could see her struggling with Josh and so agreed to her taking on a nanny for him. I didn't want to move him again. I thought eventually the tranquillity of the island would settle him. Could I have done it any better?' Daniel suddenly asked.

'I don't know, I really don't,' she admitted. 'You had to fight back in your business world for Josh's future, but...but—'

'But you think I should have done it with Josh at my side?'

'The sixty-four-million-dollar question,' Karis breathed. 'He had rejected you and it might have made it worse. All I can console you with is that Josh is responding to you now, slowly, but you've definitely made progress.'

'It's you that's made the progress with him, Karis. I dread to think of the worse state he might be in if Fiesta hadn't found you.'

'Maybe,' Karis murmured; she couldn't respond any more positively to the compliment because her heart was suddenly heavy. Daniel was going to start a new life with Simone and with Josh and Karis knew that would present new problems for the boy. Wrenched from her love and care he could so easily regress. And selfishly she thought of herself along with Josh. Daniel was mattering to her. Now she knew all about his tragic past, so much in line with her own, she felt closer to him, and it was nothing to do with sympathy. They had shared confidences, yes, but there was more. But that more was dangerous. She must keep reminding herself that it was going to be Daniel and Simone and Josh and there was no niche for her.

The soft Caribbean breeze freshened her brow and her senses. 'Thank you for telling me all this, Daniel. It isn't easy, I know, and I can't say anything that will make it any better for you. Nothing in the world can put the clock back and there is only the future after all. You must think of Josh's happiness now. He is responding to you and there will be more to come.'

Suddenly she felt very tired, exhausted in fact, drained of all emotion. 'Do you want anything to eat or drink before I go to bed?' She sounded like the hired help again—which she was, she reminded herself wearily.

He glanced at her and then at his watch. 'A bit early for bed, isn't it?'

'I didn't get much sleep with Tara last night,' she admitted with a smile. Now she sounded like a mother—which she also was, she reminded herself.

He smiled too. 'I'm going for a walk,' he told her, and leaned forward and unexpectedly kissed her tenderly on the lips.

Karis cherished the brief warmth and found to her dread that she wanted just a little more. Oh, it was so easy to entertain the romantic notion that there was a possibility of getting involved in his life. After all, she was very much a part of Josh's already. But how easy it also was to let that little boy's presence in her heart affect how she might feel for the father. She couldn't be attracted to him, she tried to convince herself.

Her love for Josh was swaying her emotions backwards and forwards and influencing her thinking surely?

Oh, she didn't know. She didn't know if it would be different if she had met Daniel Kennedy in a supermarket or on holiday or anywhere else but here on this island, with her looking after his small, frightened son. But this man was pulling at her heartstrings and one thing she was sure of was that it wasn't in sympathy for his predicament.

He stroked her chin lightly and then dropped a bombshell which Karis took as the final warning to her heart.

'I've decided to take Josh on the fishing trip with me and Simone tomorrow. I'm sure he'll enjoy it and I'm sure you could do with the break for a few days. We'll get his stuff together in the morning. Goodnight, Karis.'

Numbly she watched as he walked away, a dark, troubled silhouette against a pale moonlit sky. Moonstruck, that was what she was, moonstruck, she thought bitterly. Hadn't she learnt anything in life? Daniel had confided in her about his terrible tragic past. Daniel had kissed her. Daniel had said his heart was responding to her and Daniel had metaphorically slapped her in the face. He was taking Josh with him so his son could get to know Simone better. She bit her lip. And he was doing it for Josh and Josh might get to love Simone and...

Tight-lipped, Karis cleared the coffee-cups from the table and slammed them into the kitchen sink. Ten minutes later, after checking the children, she was in bed. But sleep didn't claim her, anxiety did. She worried about Daniel and mulled over everything he had told her. He was right; her tale of woe was nothing compared to his. But there was worse to come, she felt sure, because she was lying here, sleepless and listening for Daniel, waiting to hear if he came back or not.

And if he didn't come back it would mean he had turned

to Simone for some solace after putting himself through the torture of reliving his wife's death with his son's nanny.

Karis buried her head in the pillow so she wouldn't know if he did or didn't return. She really didn't want to know.

CHAPTER SIX

'I HATE fishing!' Josh cried passionately. 'It's cruel. It hurts them. I won't go!'

'You eat fish every day,' Saffron butted in. 'How do you think they get on your plate? They dive on?'

'That's enough, Saffron,' Daniel ordered thickly. 'Go and pack his things.'

Saffron padded out of the kitchen, giving Karis a look of sufferance on the way. Karis gave her one in return. Josh wasn't at all thrilled at the idea of the fishing trip Daniel had just told him about and Karis and Saffron were doing their best to smooth things over between father and son.

'I won't go!' Josh cried again, his face flushed with anger. 'I hate those people. I hate that lady. I hate you!' he screamed at Daniel.

The pain in Daniel's face cut Karis through to the bone. Suddenly she was helpless, not knowing what to do or say.

'Josh, please,' she whispered. 'It will be a good trip and—'

Josh turned on Karis, his face red and puckered. 'And I hate you too!' he cried bitterly, and flew from the room.

Daniel let out a groan and raked his hands through his hair. 'Dear God, but it's getting worse. Two steps forward and three back.'

'He didn't mean it.'

His eyes flashed with anger at her. 'Of course he meant it! The child is impossible. Don't make excuses for him all the time.'

'If somebody doesn't who is there for him?' Karis argued, angry herself now, slamming around the kitchen, stepping around Tara who, unperturbed by the whole business, was happily playing on the floor.

'What are you, his damned guardian angel, excusing his bad behaviour all the time? Didn't that get to you just now, him saying he hated you?'

Karis swung round and faced him, fighting her anger because of Tara at her feet.

'No, Daniel, it didn't get to me. I've heard it all before. He hated me for weeks when I arrived. Hurt and bewildered, he fought me like a wildcat. I won him over with tenderness and patience and what he said just now meant nothing because as I said he didn't mean it. He's a troubled five-year-old with a dark history and I make allowances for that. And if you had any compassion you would too. He doesn't mix very well. He's probably terrified of all those people he doesn't know. You're the one hurt because he doesn't want to go on this trip with you and suddenly it isn't softly, softly any more, it's "The child is impossible". You are the one that's impossible, Daniel!'

She stormed out of the room as Saffron came back in to gather Tara up from the floor. Daniel caught Karis on the verandah on her way to Josh's bedroom. He swung her round to face him, his face taut with anger.

'You are getting above yourself,' he said stiffly, keeping his voice low.

'Yes, I would be, wouldn't I?' she ground out defiantly. 'Last night I was superwoman, dropping pearls of wisdom, lightening your life, listening to your past and actually understanding and sympathising. This morning you want to go on a fishing trip with the stepmother from hell and I'm staff again and getting above myself and—'

He let her go and suddenly a knowing grin spread like a bush fire across his face. 'My God, you're jealous,' he breathed.

'Jealous!' Karis squawked, pink-faced and ready to throw a punch at him. 'Where did you conjure up that idea from—the joke bag?' she threw at him instead of the blow.

'Don't you try and get out of it with flippancy, Karis,' he warned, eyes dancing with mischief. 'You're jealous because Simone has got her way and I've agreed to this fishing trip. This isn't anything to do with Josh. You don't want *me* to go.'

'I am *not* jealous,' she cried, almost stamping her foot because he just wouldn't believe her. 'But if I was, which I'm not, but if—*wildly if*— it would not be a reason to argue with you over a silly boat trip. You are making an issue of everything to cover your hurt that Josh has rejected you, *again*. I'm beginning to wonder who is the bigger kid, you or Josh!'

He laughed. He actually laughed.

'You're mad,' she breathed furiously. 'The Tropics can do that to you, you know, but I suspect you were halfway there when you arrived!'

She stormed off along the verandah and angrily slid open Josh's patio door and stepped into the room before he could respond. She could still hear Daniel laughing softly as he went back along the verandah and that made her angrier still. She bit it all down, though, for Josh's sake.

Josh got up from the bed and threw himself into her arms. 'I didn't mean it, Kari—I don't hate you, I love you.'

Karis held him close, her heart thudding a million beats to the second after that row with Daniel and now Josh telling her he was sorry and he loved her. Daniel would give the world to hear those words directed at him. Oh, it was a sobering thought, one that washed away all thoughts of jealousy and angry feelings for the little boy's father at the moment.

'Oh, Josh. Your daddy wanted to take you on that trip so much and he is so disappointed that you didn't want to go with him.'

Josh tipped his tear-stained face up to look at her. His eyes were wide and distraught. She felt him tremble in her arms. He really didn't want to go and Karis prayed it was just because of his insecurity with strangers and not another rejection of his father.

'I...I...don't want to leave you. I don't want to go with that lady. She doesn't like me very much and I don't think she likes my father very much either. Can...can you come with us? I'll go if you come, Kari.'

Karis sat down on the edge of the bed and pulled him to her, stroking his hair. He didn't want to leave her and how those words hurt. One day, and quite soon too, he would have to leave her and it would be for good. She wondered how he would cope with that and she felt guilty for not thinking of him before. Always she had wondered how *she* was going to cope with losing him, but how would Josh cope with losing her? She couldn't begin to imagine. She couldn't begin to imagine Simone taking her place in his heart. The thought was terrifying.

'I haven't been asked,' she told him soothingly, trying so hard to pacify him. 'And if I had been I couldn't leave Tara.'

'You can,' Josh insisted sulkily. 'Saffron will have her and then we can all go,' he suggested, as if Tara were an inanimate object to be dumped on Saffron.

Before Karis could think of an answer to that Daniel stepped into the room. On sight of him Josh buried his head in Karis's arms and Karis soothed him by stroking his hair. She looked up at Daniel and silently appealed to him to be gentle with the boy.

'The trip's off, I'm afraid, Josh,' Daniel said quietly. 'Trouble with the engines, I believe. None of us can go,' he added.

Wide-eyed, Karis gazed at him over the top of Josh's dark head. Their eyes met and neither looked away because there was such a depth of understanding between them, a sudden conspiratorial closeness that made her feel ashamed for her outburst earlier.

There was no way he could have got over to the house and back with that information. He was lying because Josh couldn't be seen to triumph over his father's wishes though that was exactly what had happened. Daniel understood that it would cause pain to his son to insist on him going on the trip, so he was being diplomatic. Karis wondered if he had overheard their conversation and was saving her embarrassment too. No way would she be asked to go on the trip because she was considered staff.

'To make up for it why don't we all go to the creek?' Daniel suggested. 'I think it's time Karis started giving me those diving lessons, don't you, Josh?'

Slowly Josh lifted his head. He sniffed loudly and rubbed at his nose before allowing a small smile to brighten his face. It was the only gesture he would allow to indicate his agreement.

Karis gave Daniel a small smile too and it was the only gesture *she* would allow to indicate *her* agreement. Because of Josh they were forced into calling a truce.

'I said he would be hopeless, didn't I? Karis laughed, clutching Josh's hand as they stood watching Daniel cringing on the top of the rock, making a terrible to-do about leaping into the water below.

'He's teasing,' Josh cried with excitement. 'He can do it! He can!'

Karis cupped her hand to the side of her mouth and called out to Daniel, 'Your secret is out. You're nothing but an impostor. Josh says you're teasing.'

Daniel shrugged his broad shoulders and then flexed himself and did the most appalling belly-flop into the water, then spluttered as his head came up from the foam around him, overacting like mad.

Josh shrieked with laughter, jumping up and down and squeezing Karis's hand so hard it hurt.

It was a breakthrough, Karis felt as Daniel swam towards them. Josh was giggling so hard he was embarrassing himself and he hid behind Karis's bare legs. Karis would have loved to see Josh rush into the water to greet his father as he always did her when she dived off the rock. But it was progress that his father had made him laugh.

'You were right, Josh. I am an impostor. That was a perfect dive, wasn't it?'

'It wasn't! It wasn't!' Josh cried, coming out from behind Karis. 'You were teasing again. You can do it. I know you can.'

'Can't fool you for a minute, can I?' Daniel laughed, raking his wet hair from his face.

And he couldn't fool Karis either. It was obvious by the light in his eyes and the grin on his face that it gave him enormous pleasure to be able to make his son laugh.

Later, after taking a very slow amble back from the creek, Karis lay sprawled under the sun umbrella on the beach near the cottage. Lying on her front with her chin propped on her arms, she watched Daniel and Josh beachcombing. Softly, softly. Daniel hadn't been lulled into a false sense of security by Josh's hysterics at his diving performance and he wasn't going overboard with the boy now. He had simply taken off along the beach saying he was going to look for shells and Josh had simply joined him of his own accord a few minutes later.

'I should be happy for them both,' she murmured to herself as she got up and gathered up the towels. 'And I am.' But she wasn't happy for herself. Daniel and Josh's tentative bonding meant the very worst for Karis. The loss of Josh. It bit into her heart, her soul; every part of her was painfully preparing for the final wrench. She wouldn't be able to bear it when the time came. And now there was a new sadness waiting to be heaped on her. Daniel too would go.

'I'm going back to the cottage,' she called out, but neither of them heard her over the rippling rush of water on the shore and Karis felt a shiver of loneliness run down her spine.

'How is she?' Karis asked Saffron when she got back to the cottage. Saffron had insisted on keeping Tara in the relative cool of the cottage while they went to the creek. The weather was ever more humid, heat pressing down on heat.

'Sleeping,' Saffron told her from the cane chair she was rocking to and fro on the verandah, fanning herself with a palm leaf. 'Where's Josh?'

'Still on the beach with his father.' Karis flopped down in another chair and brushed the sand from her feet.

'Huh,' snorted Saffron, swishing her makeshift fan impatiently.

'He's making progress,' Karis insisted, defending Daniel from that snort of derision. Saffron didn't see the half of what she saw—the gentle persuasion in Daniel's treatment of the boy. 'Daniel really loves him, you know, and Josh is responding to him. Deep down he really loves him but he can't admit it yet.'

'Yeah, and like somebody else I know,' Saffron drawled.

'Yes, well, Simone—'

'I don't mean no swanky woman from the pleasure palace,' she cut in. 'I means you, girl.'

Hot and fazed at that remark, Karis stared at her hard. Her heart started to pump erratically. 'What on earth?'

'Don't you deny it 'cos I won't believe it. I have eyes and I can see you.'

'Saffron!' Karis exploded warningly, her heart thundering so hard now she could almost hear it as well as feel it.

Saffron grinned, rocking to and fro, all-knowing.

'I sees the way you looks at him and the way he looks at you. Josh will see it soon and then there'll be trouble.'

'Trouble?' Karis husked, her head spinning.

'Trouble if you don't marry that man and be Josh's mother like he treats you now.'

Karis got to her feet, every nerve-ending screaming. Her legs felt like jelly, hardly able to support her. That wasn't possible. Not in Saffron's wildest dreams and not in her own. Daniel was committed to another. He wasn't available and Saffron was very wrong in thinking the way he looked at her and she looked at him meant anything. They had just reached a mutual understanding, that was all. All for Josh. And as for Josh, he knew she wasn't his mother and if he leaned on her at times it was...it was because she had cared for him so well and there was no chance, none whatsoever, that things could be any different than they were. Daniel was going to marry Simone and take Josh home to the States.

Inwardly trembling, hands visibly shaking, Karis glared at Saffron. She wanted to tear into her for that, to cry that she should know her place and mind her own business, but she couldn't. Saffron had been too good a friend in the past.

'You're impossible,' was all she could feebly mutter before storming off along the verandah. Everyone was impossible!

Karis pulled off her bikini and wrapped a batik sarong around her before throwing herself on her bed and beating hell out of her pillow. What was she doing here? She had come to escape and now...now she wanted to escape again, run for her life because suddenly that life was more impossible than ever. She loved a man she couldn't have, she loved a child she couldn't have...

'Oh, no,' she moaned, in complete and utter misery. I *don't* love Daniel, she reasoned determinedly, giving her pillow another beating. I'm simply emotionally torn by the whole situation, wanting the best for Josh, and...and the best for Josh is to be with his father and that is how it is going to be and there is no place for me in their lives.

Karis sat up and hugged her knees tightly and stared blindly at the white walls of her bedroom. All-knowing Saffron had seen the way she looked at him. Were her feelings so open to scrutiny? Oh, she would have to be so, so careful because if Saffron could see then Daniel surely might and that would mean trouble.

But Saffron couldn't have read anything in the way Daniel looked at her. Daniel saw her the way Fiesta saw her—as Josh's carer. He might have teased her, he might have kissed her, all little ploys to keep her sweet and in her place, but Saffron hadn't been witness to any of those games. No, Saffron was wrong to think he looked at her in any special way. So very wrong.

'What's wrong?'

Karis jumped as if she had been shot. Daniel stood in the doorway, barefoot, wearing shorts and with a cool silk shirt hanging loosely over the top, his dark, glossy hair tousled as if he'd just rubbed it with a towel. In a fleeting second it struck Karis that he too was going native lately. She jumped up from the bed and smoothed down her sarong. 'I'd better see to the children,' she muttered hurriedly.

'Forget the children for a minute. What's wrong? Saffron said you'd gone to your room vexed.'

I'll kill her, Karis ground out inwardly. If anyone was getting above themselves it was Saffron. Good God, if she told Daniel what she had said to her...

'Of course I'm not vexed,' she denied vehemently. 'I have a headache, that's all. The rains are coming—'

'You don't look in pain.'

'What do you know?' she snapped at him, and went to brush past him.

He stopped her, grasped at her arm and swung her to face him. His face was dark with anger.

'I know enough to know you aren't suffering from a headache. Now give; what's wrong?'

'Nothing's wrong,' she insisted angrily. 'Can't I have five minutes to myself without the whole world questioning it?'

His brow furrowed. 'Are you still mad at me for teasing you about being jealous of Simone?'

'Oh, don't be ridiculous, Daniel. I forgot that hours ago.'

'This is all getting too much for you, isn't it? Me and Josh, the extra work involved, the child's tantrums—'

'No, Daniel,' she blurted. Her shoulders softened under his grip. 'Everything is fine,' she assured him, her anger abated now. 'You and Josh, you're doing just fine, and...and—'

She swallowed hard. The very nearness of him was making her crumble. His warm hands, so firm and yet gentle, were still holding her shoulders and it was very nearly too much for her. She wanted to tear away but couldn't because of this awful weakness melting her very bones. Her eyelashes fluttered as she looked up at him, willing herself to be strong and somehow get out of this room before she gave something away.

'I'm...I'm just tired.'

Bone-weary if the truth be known. It flooded her now, the sheer exhaustion of battling with her emotions. Every day since he had come she had waged some sort of war with her senses. He was right, it was getting too much for her, but his reasons weren't right. It wasn't to do with him and Josh, just him.

She stepped back, afraid now that he might see what she was fighting to control.

'I don't believe you,' he told her. 'I think it's me troubling you.'

Her breath caught in her throat. She held it there. He couldn't know.

'It's what I told you last night,' he added.

Her breath came back. She let it out with a small explosion. 'Look, I didn't care about that trip with Simone—'

He grasped her again, nearly shook her this time. 'I'm not talking about Simone. I'm talking about what I told you about Josh's mother and my marriage. It's affected you—'

'It has not!' Karis retorted, though she was secretly relieved he thought that was what was bothering her. She struggled free of him and stood her ground in front of him. 'The past is the past, Daniel, at times to be forgotten for the sake of sanity. Honestly, did you really think after all I've been through in *my* past I wouldn't understand? That says a lot for me, doesn't it? Heavens, if it had affected me I wouldn't have been out swimming with you in the creek this morning, especially after our row.'

'And we had a good time,' he uttered with a very small smile, 'all of us, and then suddenly you go all vexed—'

'You're beginning to sound like the locals.' She laughed at him, trying so very hard to play everything down.

'I'm beginning to sound like someone caring too much,' he admitted softly. 'Your moods affect me, Karis; they affect everyone. You are one powerful lady if you did but know it.'

Karis nearly laughed out loud at that but she wasn't allowed any form of amusement. His mouth suddenly swooped down to hers and his lips on hers were crushing in their intensity. He pulled her against his hard body, shocking her with the arousal it betrayed. Deeper and deeper went the kiss, draining her of all sane will in her body. He was so powerful and she...she wasn't powerful at all, nothing but soft submission, fighting it but hopelessly losing it.

She felt his hand move up to her chest, her all-betraying breasts straining against the flimsy cotton of her sarong. Her head swam with the dizzy sensation of having them caressed, his thumb running over the raised nubs, driving her wild with despair. She wanted him to stop the ecstatic assault and yet she wanted more.

Her lips parted, weakly allowing him an intimacy she knew she ought to stop. Her whole body flamed in his arms and he knew and groaned softly against her as if he too was pulling up a battle that was hopelessly lost. She felt a soft tug at the knot of her sarong and then pressure, his fingers cupping her naked flesh, moulding her in his hand—soft, soft pressure of electrifying intensity.

A small moan escaped her swollen lips and his mouth moved away, down, down the long column of her heated throat to the perfumed hollow at its base. She drew in her lower lip as his mouth brushed the sensitive rise of her breasts and then his tongue snaked tantalisingly across her nipple and she felt the heat of desire spread to every nerve-ending in her body.

With a sob she pulled back, grasping at his shoulders to hold him off. The sarong slid down to the floor between them and the panic of being naked and so vulnerable in front of him powered the last vestige of strength to her melting bones.

She let him go, panic darkening her eyes. She tried to squat to retrieve the scrap of cloth that would save her dignity but he caught her wrists. His eyes were heavy with the desire she had so abruptly tried to put an end to, his mouth tight and controlled.

'No,' he breathed. 'Let me see you.'

'No, Daniel,' she whispered desperately, her eyes wide and pleading. 'This is all wrong and...please, no.'

Her plea went unanswered as he shifted her a pace back from him and spread her arms wide so he could devour every inch of her heated body with his hungry eyes. The scrutiny was so painful that Karis closed herself off from it. She squeezed her eyes shut and a clamp came around her heart, holding it back, not allowing it to race as crazily as it wanted.

He let go of her wrists and touched her then, both hands

smoothing down her body, down to her waist, the slight rounding of her hips, the feather-light caresses of admiration tingling her flesh till she was swamped by a desire to fall into his arms and let whatever might be be.

'I repeat myself,' he murmured throatily, 'and make no apologies for it. Your husband was a fool. He should have been overjoyed you were carrying his child. He had it all and let it go.'

Karis fluttered open her eyes and saw something that filled her with such awe that she didn't know whether to allow fear or joy to enter her heart. His eyes held hers, the hunger in them so starkly apparent it brought shivers to her rigid spine. He wanted her and there was sheer determination in the steely glint that told her he would do everything in his power to satisfy that hunger.

She parted her lips, not sure of what was going to come out but needing to make some sort of protest or even utter a warning because this was all wrong. He stilled her lips with a thumb, the small, soothing pressure stopping her from uttering a single breathy word.

'But you won't escape me, Karis, and you won't try because you don't want to.'

Did he expect a denial? She stepped back then—a denial, if not spoken. Bravely she scooped her sarong from the floor and had it around her body before he could stop her. Though he didn't try. He didn't have to because he had seen it all. Her nakedness, her vulnerability, her weakness, and very probably her heated desire for him. She needed time and he was going to give it to her but he didn't know that he was very wrong. She *would* escape him. She couldn't get off this island but she could escape him emotionally. All she had to do was remind herself that his fiancée was but a few hundred yards from here, his son closer, her daughter closer still. She had her defences, all three of them if all else failed.

'I have to see to the children,' she murmured, trying to bring some authority to her tone but suspecting she had failed miserably because he simply smiled at her.

'Of course, the children. Let's not forget the children.'

He was gone before she could fully analyse that slightly mocking tone to his voice. Had he actually struck into her mind, reading those defences she was preparing to use? Impossible. He wasn't psychic.

'You've done what?'

Karis gaped in astonishment. She'd busied herself all afternoon, doing trivial jobs around the cottage while the children were taking their siesta. Anything and everything to keep her mind off Daniel Kennedy. Saffron had gone back to her own cottage. Daniel had gone somewhere, possibly to see Simone off on her fishing trip because he had lied to Josh and the trip wasn't off. Now he was back, smiling at her across the kitchen after landing another of his bombshells.

'Saffron asked my permission and I gave it because it falls in very nicely with my plans for the evening. The children will enjoy the party and be in safe hands and we are going to be free for the evening.'

'Free to do what?' she asked idiotically, so taken aback she couldn't think straight.

'To go out.'

'Out? Out where? There's nowhere to go!' she blustered. The heat and humidity had surely gone to his head.

'I thought a barbecue on the beach would be nice. Just us and the stars and the moon.'

Karis turned her back on him, making a poor job of filling the ice trays for the freezer. Her hands were shaking so badly the water spilled every time she moved. This was a conspiracy, inspired by Saffron, no doubt, to get them alone together. How could she have gone behind her back and arranged this with

Daniel? It was cruel. And why was Daniel taking all this so far, bewitching her with a promise of a night of stars? He was cruel, using her...yes, using her because Simone wasn't here.

'Tara isn't going to no party,' she fumed.

'That's a double negative,' he responded, and she knew he would still be grinning.

She whirled on him. 'Oh, excuse my grammar,' she grated sarcastically. 'I stand corrected. Tara isn't going to *the* party. And here's another double negative. No, no!'

He came and took the ice tray from her and slammed it down into the sink. He wasn't smiling any more.

'I won't take no for an answer, Karis. If you want to get stroppy about this I'll remind you I pay the wages around here.'

'Back to that again, are we?' she sniped. 'Can't you think of anything more original? Anyway, *you* can't tell me what to do with my own child!'

'No, I can't. But Josh is going to the party because I say so,' he emphasised firmly. 'And Josh wants to go and he'll want Tara to go and Saffron wants Tara to go—'

'*I* don't want her to go and I'm her mother in case you have forgotten!' Karis stated firmly, her eyes determined.

'You don't want her to go because you are using her as an excuse not to be alone with me for the night.'

Karis thought she was going to explode with indignation. Yes, very true but how dared he know that? Her eyes changed from determined to incredulous, as if the very idea were impossible.

'I'm right, Karis,' Daniel insisted. 'You knew about this party a long while ago and didn't object. Saffron said you had agreed.'

Damn! She had forgotten and now here she was making a scene because she thought it had been a plan cooked up by Saffron to get them alone, really alone together. She remembered Saffron had mentioned her little niece's birthday party arrangements before Daniel had arrived on the island. The staff often had parties in their own cottage complex, wonderful parties with singing and dancing and calypso. The West Indians adored their children and the parties were always fun. Josh had been to one before and it had been one of the few occasions when he had socialised well.

'I'd forgotten,' she reluctantly conceded, and lowered her lashes and hoped that it would be excuse enough for him and he wouldn't pursue the idea that she was objecting on the grounds of being afraid of spending an evening alone with him now that Simone was out of the way.

'We need some time on our own, Karis,' he told her softly.

Karis widened her eyes in objection, heat rushing to her face.

'You sound like a husband and a father and I wish you hadn't said that, Daniel,' she rushed out. 'Because it very much sounds as if because Simone is out of the way you feel free to...to—'

'To pursue you?' he interjected quickly, his eyes burning. 'Is that what you think—that I've got Simone out of the way so I can pursue you?'

'Haven't you?'

His eyes narrowed dangerously and he stepped towards her. Karis backed off but came up against a work surface far too soon. She gripped it behind her, willing it to give her strength if she needed it. He stopped in front of her, dangerously close.

'I think it is time you accepted that there is something between us to be pursued, Karis,' he breathed, as if it was a warning.

Karis ran her tongue over her bottom lip. He had this effect on her, rushing her nerves till she barely had the ability to swallow.

'Tonight, under the stars, you might begin to realise that

some things can't be fought. If I can put Simone out of my mind then so can you.'

But she wasn't him, someone without scruples. He talked of the woman he was considering marriage to as if she didn't matter!

'No, I can't,' she uttered at last, lifting her chin. 'You're nothing but an opportunist. It's all worked out beautifully for you, hasn't it? This children's party tonight, Simone sailing the high seas a million starry miles away from here. Well, out of sight, out of mind doesn't apply to me, Daniel. I recognise that you have problems with your relationship with Simone but I'm not the way out for you.'

His dark brows came up in surprise. 'You think I'm using you to rid myself of Simone? Playing some sort of play-off game?'

Actually it hadn't crossed her mind. The statement had just come out instinctively as some form of defence, the last straw to clutch at.

'I'm not clever or devious enough to think that way, Daniel. But the fact that you jumped on it so heatedly suggests the idea *had* crossed your mind.'

He laughed, one of those derisory laughs weighted with disbelief.

'You have an uncanny knack of turning the tables on me, Karis, sweetheart. But let me put you straight on a few matters. I'm not devious either. I've told you before that Simone and I have an understanding. If things don't work out we go our own ways.'

Karis gripped the surface behind her. Her insides felt curiously wobbly.

'And...and what is that supposed to mean?' she asked in a small voice.

'It means exactly what I said. If it doesn't work out we go our separate ways. Marriage is a tricky business, as you well know. The romantic notion that it is based on love doesn't guarantee its success. There is far more to it. In spite of what you have seen of us together Simone and I had a lot going for us. We have known each other a long time. I knew her before I knew my wife. Both of us have had disastrous relationships before and we'd talked all this through. We knew the pitfalls. This trip served a double purpose. It was mainly for Josh and the rest was for Simone and I to make a firm decision on our future together.'

Karis's breath wouldn't come. She felt all choked up inside. This was further confirmation that he didn't love Simone and now it was sounding as if she didn't love him either. A marriage of convenience and poor little Josh in the middle of it all. It was unthinkable.

Her breath came back and the tightness in her chest eased. 'What sort of people are you?' she breathed hotly. 'You don't love each other and yet you are considering marriage. You have an arrangement that if it doesn't work out you walk away. It sounds more like a business deal than a relationship.'

'I felt that there was no other option at the time,' he told her gravely. 'I wanted to make it good for Josh. Don't you understand the motivation behind it? My son is the most important person to me. I owe him and sometimes personal sacrifices have to be made. Like you, I have ideals, but sometimes they are unobtainable and you have to take the next best thing. Simone and I could have worked it out to make a life for us all but—'

He stopped suddenly and Karis stared at him because she had listened intently, soaked up every word and suddenly they were making sense. He had been speaking in the past tense, as if he and Simone had already made the decision *not* to go ahead.

She felt dizzy talking about it. But perhaps she hadn't heard right; perhaps she had misinterpreted it because it was what she wanted to hear.

Daniel cleared his throat. 'So we go ahead with tonight's arrangements,' he said stiffly. 'The children go to the party and we relax and have some time to ourselves. Do you have any problem with that?'

A million, she wanted to say, but because she was still puzzling over all he had said about him and Simone she decided a close guard on her feelings would be for the best.

She lifted her chin and told him tightly, 'There is no problem, just so long as you remember that you pay my wages, as you are so inclined to remind me now and then. All should be well if we stick to the rules. You my employer, me the expendable one.'

He smiled and shook his dark head as if he couldn't believe her at times. 'I doubt all will be well till you spirit yourself out into the real world, Karis. You've lived too long coiled in the protection of a magic lamp. Watch out for Aladdin tonight.'

He left her breathless and puzzled in the kitchen. So he was about to free her, was he? He was the one living in an unreal world. He'd find out tonight if he dared to try and work his magic on her. If he wanted a pantomime he'd soon find out she wasn't Widow Twanky!

CHAPTER SEVEN

'OH, SAFFRON,' Karis breathed with pleasure. 'It's gorgeous. She looks wonderful. Look, Daniel. Isn't Saffron clever? She's made Tara a party dress.'

'Amazing,' Daniel agreed, leaning forward in Saffron's rocker on the verandah and holding his hands out to Tara who toddled towards him laughing happily. 'Come on, treasure, give us a twirl so we can see how beautiful you look.'

The dress was sunshine-yellow with a mass of frills at the tiny sleeves and hem. The bodice was embroidered with tiny flowers and glass beads. Saffron had tied her dark curly hair up on her head with a yellow satin ribbon and the ends spiralled down her back. It was a fun party outfit, frothy and extravagant and very Caribbean.

Daniel held her hands and turned her around so they could all see the big satin bow tied behind her back. Tara giggled and rose to the occasion, showing off until she toppled and Daniel swept her up onto his lap.

'And next,' Saffron cooed. 'Come on, Josh, out from those shadows and show your papa your new outfit.'

Daniel threw Karis an agonised glance which she returned with one of her own. If Saffron had decked Josh out so extravagantly the boy would cringe with embarrassment.

Josh stepped out of the shadows with a tentative grin on his face, not sure if he liked being paraded or not.

'Oh, Josh, you look so grown-up,' breathed Karis, half in relief, half in genuine admiration. She flashed a quick look at Daniel and his eyes reflected equal relief.

Josh wore long white trousers—his first. His shirt was crisp white too, short-sleeved with a narrow band of yellow at the edge—the same fabric as Tara's dress. A very conservative frill of matching yellow ran down the front of the shirt. At his waist was a yellow satin cummerbund. Saffron had put some sort of gel on his usually tousled dark hair and combed it back from his forehead.

'Josh, you look marvellous, immaculate,' Daniel enthused. 'Come here. Let me see you together.'

Still holding Tara on his lap, he held his other hand out to Josh. Josh looked shyly at him and then crossed the verandah and stood in front of his father. He didn't take Daniel's outstretched hand, though; instead he reached for Tara's and held it as if drawing confidence from her.

Karis felt a lump in her throat. The sight of Daniel with her daughter on his lap and his son holding the little girl's hand was very moving.

'You got a camera, Mr Kennedy? You should have a picture of you all.'

Karis glowered at Saffron, knowing what she was trying to do, but Saffron looked so innocent she wondered if she was mistaken.

Nevertheless Karis said, 'I have,' and scooted along to her bedroom to get it. She'd taken several films since coming to Levos, none of them developed yet, all in store in the fridge. She only fleetingly thought that when she left here she'd have them developed and put herself through agonies looking at them.

She held the camera in her hand and stared at it and the fleeting thought she had just dismissed leapt back at her with a vengeance. This film would make her suffer the worst. Daniel would be on it, and Josh and Tara, and it would be unbearable to look at them after Daniel and Josh had left, unbearable. Bravely Karis willed herself into planting a smile on her face and returning to the verandah where everyone was waiting.

'Here, let me do it,' Saffron said, and took the camera from her. 'You stand behind them, Miss Karis.'

Karis took up her position behind the group and tried to look comfortable about the whole business. She wasn't, though; it was awful trying to hide her angst. It would look like a family group and it wasn't but to object would spoil the evening for everyone.

'The other end,' Daniel laughed, and Josh laughed with him as Saffron turned the unfamiliar camera around in her hands.

The flash lightening the darkness around them sent Tara into fits of giggles and Josh laughed and pulled at her hand, urging her down from his father's lap.

Karis wondered if Josh was jealous. If he was it would show a feeling for his father. Jealousy was a positive response in some cases, she thought ruefully.

'Saffron said she used the same material for our clothes so people would think we were brother and sister,' Josh said as he knelt to adjust the rumpled frills at Tara's hem.

Karis gave Saffron a dark look. She shouldn't be putting ideas into his head.

'You do look like brother and sister,' Daniel agreed.

And Karis gave Saffron an even darker look. She shouldn't be putting ideas into Daniel's head either.

'Come on, you two; let's get to the party before the jelly melts,' Saffron suggested, handing the camera back to Karis.

She hoisted Tara up onto her ample hip and reached for Josh's hand. He went to Karis, though, and lifted his arms for a hug and a kiss goodbye and then went to his father. Karis held her breath. He paused slightly before extending his right hand formally to Daniel. Daniel looked at his son for what seemed like for ever to Karis. His eyes looked pained, as if he was disappointed his son hadn't given him the same fond farewell he'd given to Karis. He took his son's hand and shook it and when Josh turned away to take Saffron's outstretched hand Karis saw a flush on the boy's face and a very small smile at the corner of his mouth.

'The presents,' Karis said quickly, feeling the pain of Daniel's disappointment and trying to cover it for them both. 'You nearly forgot the presents, Josh.'

She gathered up the gaily wrapped gifts from the table. After siesta she and Josh had scoured the toy cupboard for something suitable. There were no shops on the island so something new wasn't possible. Josh had wanted to give Saffron's niece the robot Simone had given him but Karis had persuaded him it wasn't suitable for a four-year-old girl. They'd found a new box of crayons Josh hadn't used and a doll that Karis had bought for Tara in St Lucia, meaning to keep it for her next birthday, and Josh had painted a card and stuck shells on it. He'd helped wrap the presents too and Karis had been thrilled by his enthusiasm.

Karis stood by the verandah rail and waved them off through the lit gardens, Saffron singing a calypso and Josh joining in in the bits that he knew. Karis turned to Daniel and was dismayed to see him with his head in his hands.

The silence was as heavy as the heat around them. A gecko scuttled up the wall and a candle flickered and Karis at last broke the silence. 'Don't be disappointed, Daniel,' she said softly. 'He'll get around to giving you a hug very soon. The handshake is a start.'

Daniel let his hands drop and lifted his face to look at her. The pain was so obvious in his eyes that she knew no words of consolation could ease his suffering.

'We used to do that when he was no more than Tara's age,' he told her thickly. 'It was a game, shaking hands like grown men. I didn't think he remembered that far back. He must remember it all. The night his mother died. He could have heard her cry out—Oh, God, it's all still with him, buried so deep inside—'

'Don't, Daniel, don't,' she pleaded. Without thinking she dropped to her knees and took his hand and squeezed it tightly. 'Not everything; he wouldn't remember everything. Children don't; they are so resilient at times we could learn a lesson from them. Yes, he remembered the handshake and that is wonderful, not sad. He remembered something good, a game you played, and that was his way of reminding you, just in case you had forgotten.'

He lifted her hand over his and kissed it lightly and when he looked at her he was smiling. 'You're wonderful,' he whispered. 'Too good to be true.'

Embarrassed and touched, Karis stood up. He caught her hand and when she looked down at him he said, 'Our time now, Karis, and God forbid that Saffron has made you a party dress too.'

The joke eased the tension and they laughed together and Karis was still smiling as she went to get ready. They had both agreed Tara had looked like something off the top of the Christmas tree and Josh like a trainee waiter for a mini-tots' restaurant. But Saffron had made the children happy and they both appreciated her efforts, though only Karis knew the scale of her effort in making the children look like brother and sister. She must have plotted that ages ago, even before she had known how Karis felt about Daniel. Cunning Saffron. Tomorrow Karis would have to have words with her...

But tonight she wanted to forget tomorrow. Tonight was for them, no children, no shadows from the past, just the night. A barbecue under the stars with Daniel. It would be what she made it, nothing more and nothing less.

But as Karis showered and dressed, taking great care over her appearance, a sort of panic started to creep over her. It was only a barbecue on the beach but they would be alone, completely and utterly alone, and he had made it clear he desired her and she knew how she felt too.

The evening would be fizzing with danger. She could feel it now, the thrill of his touch when he had caressed her breasts... Karis shivered and frowned. If he kissed her... He would of course, she thought, and when he did would she want more? After being an emotion-weary widow for so long, would she be able to control her emotions and feelings long enough to summon flight to her boneless legs? Did she want to?

She gazed at herself in the mirror. What had Saffron seen in her eyes when she looked at Daniel? Did you wear the look of love on your face and not know it? She looked flushed, that was for sure. She glanced down at her small hands. They were shaking slightly. Nerves, excitement? She felt peculiar, wobbly inside like a teenager on a first date. But she wasn't a teenager, she reminded herself, and started to giggle. She was a widow getting ready for a date with a widower...and that sounded as if they were in their dotage!

Daniel burst out laughing when she appeared on the verandah.

'Karis, you are priceless. I refuse to take you out like that. Come here.'

Laughing, she stepped towards him. For fun she'd massed the remains of the ribbon she had wrapped the parcels with in her hair, scooping it all to the top of her head as Saffron had done to Tara. For good measure she had thrust a handful of yellow hibiscus flowers into the mass of dark hair.

Daniel loosened the ribbons and let her hair tumble to her shoulders. 'Just like I first saw you,' he murmured. 'Wild and unkempt, warmed by the tropical sun, untouched by civilisation.'

'You make me sound like Girl Friday.' She laughed hesitantly.

'You make me feel like Robinson Crusoe—haven't seen a woman in years,' he growled wolfishly.

She laughed with him. 'Well, this will crush your ardor; Romeo and Juliet we ain't. What we are are single parents snatching a few hours of respite, and if that doesn't bring you down to earth with a bump nothing will,' she teased.

'For that fearful reminder you will pay a penance,' he told her, and smiled, lifting her chin to look into her eyes. 'And it will cost you dearly, Karis,' he murmured before brushing his lips lightly across hers.

Then he took her hand and led her through the gardens to the beach and Karis thought he was probably right—it would cost her dearly and she would probably willingly pay.

She smelt the wood burning before she saw the barbecue. They stepped out onto the moonlit beach and Karis caught her breath in her throat. What she saw beside the gently smoking barbecue was astonishing.

'Oh, Daniel,' she breathed, 'it's beautiful. I'm overwhelmed.'

She gazed in awe at the table set for two under a leaning palm tree. A long white damask cloth hung down to the sand and was set with silver and crystal and fine china. A candle in a bowl with hibiscus flowers floating around it sat at the centre. The crystal sparkled and the silver glowed and it looked perfectly romantic. And not without Saffron's help, Karis felt sure. It all came from the main house; there were no such luxuries as damask, crystal and silver and bone china at the cottage.

'Like a true Caribbean pirate I plundered all of this,' he told her, squashing the Saffron theory for her. 'While the cat is away the mice shall play.'

'Fiesta will have you hung, drawn and quartered for this,' Karis warned him with humour.

'Worth it, don't you think?'

He held a chair out for her, one of a pair of exquisite French Louis the fourteenth's Karis had seen in Fiesta's sumptuous dining room; the other sat at the other side of the table, both of them with their beautifully gilded legs sunk inches into the powdery sand.

'Oh, Daniel,' Karis whispered with concern as she sat down. 'You shouldn't have gone to all this trouble. Heavens, if the sand does damage to these priceless antiques Fiesta will go crazy with rage.'

'No, she won't. I won't allow her to. The stars were a bit of a problem, I must admit. They were reluctant to come out to play tonight. I had a job and a half coaxing them out.' He looked up and Karis followed his eyes. Stars sparkled overhead in a cloudless sky.

Karis grinned at him. 'Divine intervention, more like.'

'Yes, I made a bargain with the gods. My soul for the stars.'

'Thank you,' murmured Karis, her eyes misty as she watched him take champagne from an ice bucket and pop the cork.

'You know, it's considered terribly bad form to pop a champagne cork,' he told her. 'You're supposed to soundlessly ease it off but I think it takes the fun out of it, don't you?'

I *do* love him, she thought. Hopelessly, completely, utterly. She loved him more for this because it showed his romanticism. A man who did this had to be romantic. How could he have ever considered marriage to Simone on such a cold, calculated basis? But he had said, hadn't he? That it was all for Josh, only for Josh. And now he was here, doing this for her, and he wasn't doing it for Josh. This was for her and him. Respite, romanticism, some fun? She didn't care. She was experiencing it and enjoying it and for the moment little else mattered.

'Don't you agree?'

Karis blinked and smiled. Champagne corks, she recalled.

'Yes, I agree. The louder the better.' The louder her heart beat, the champagne cork of her soul. She laughed suddenly as Daniel poured the frothy wine. The stars had gone to her head and she hadn't even drunk the wine yet.

'What can I do to help?' she asked as Daniel raked the hot ashes.

'Nothing with this. Barbecues are men's work. You can take that bowl of salad out of the cold box, though.'

Karis did it while Daniel threw the steaks onto the grill. They sizzled and threw sparks into the night and the smell was delicious. She set the bowl of salad on the table and sat sipping her champagne, suddenly at a loss for words and wondering if any were needed.

'I always thought these leaning palms grew this way because of the wind,' she began eventually, some minutes later. 'But they don't, you know. They lean over towards the sea so that when they drop their seeds, the coconuts or whatever, they are carried out on the tide and onto some distant shore, so propagating their species far and wide.'

Suddenly he was behind her and gently drawing her up from her chair. He gathered her into his arms and kissed her so tenderly she wondered what she had said to make him do it. But perhaps it was just the magic of the night affecting him as it was affecting her. The stars, the moon, the heat of a tropical night. Such things turned the mind. When at last he released her she felt weak and senseless, with only a smidgen of desire to fight it. With a knowing smile he turned back to the grill and Karis sat down and waited and wished away all thoughts but to enjoy this evening.

'Are you hungry?' he asked, taking her plate to the grill to dish up the steaks.

She was and she wasn't. How could you be hungry for food when love took your appetite away?

'Starving,' she admitted. She must be for his sake. He had gone to such trouble.

'Good. Me too.'

He sat down across from her and topped up their champagne glasses and held his aloft.

'What shall we toast?'

Karis shrugged. Josh's future might be nice to toast to but tonight wasn't about Josh. She sensed that bringing the children into the conversation would bring the night down from its magical height.

'What about us?' Daniel suggested, and held her green eyes in the candle-glow.

Karis held her glass up nervously. And what about us? she thought miserably. Where is all this going to end? The night was perfect, too perfect, too worrying, too dangerous. And would be spoiled if she didn't take it for what it was—an act of appreciation from Daniel, surely?

'Yes, us,' she said brightly, resolving to make the very best of it, for Daniel's sake.

'To us, then,' Daniel agreed, his tone so low and seductive that she wished with all her heart that the world would disappear from around them and leave them isolated in this pocket of warm sensuality.

'Oh, I nearly forgot,' Daniel leapt up and Karis watched in astonishment as he hauled a portable cassette player from the shadows and snapped it on. The theme from a romantic film softly filled the air and Karis's heart raced.

'Don't you think you are going over the top?' she said with a teasing smile.

'I went over the top the day I set foot on this island, Karis,' he told her. 'Now eat before your steak spoils.'

And Karis did. The food was wonderful and the champagne superb and she wanted time to stand still. They talked softly about mundane things like food and wine. They steered clear of children talk, past lives, the future. Later, when the moon hung low and silvery in the sky, Daniel took her in his arms and they danced.

The champagne had gone to Karis's head and she floated in his arms, he holding her so tenderly as if never to let her go. She didn't want him to, not ever. She didn't want to think. She wanted this delicious numbness to be with her for ever, this living for the moment with senses dulled. Then her senses were awakened as his mouth sought hers and she was past reasoning any more.

His lips parted hers and she clung to him, swaying slightly to the music, moving with him as his hands moved over her silk dress, smoothing the fine fabric against her skin. A delicious erotic sensation engulfed her at the pressure of the silk grazing her fiery skin, the silk being moved by him a seduction, a temptation.

'Karis,' he murmured adoringly as he nuzzled her hair. 'You can't escape me now.'

The words came through a haze, sobering her slightly. Her eyelids were heavy with desire but she struggled to lift the weight from them. Escape. This island had been her refuge. A place where she could re-evaluate her life, forget the past and make a new start. She didn't want to have to do it again, not ever. It had been too hard a struggle to throw it all away for...for a night of magic.

She drew back from him, and was suddenly very afraid. Love was fearful and should be fearless. Daniel made her feel wanted but could she give herself to him when there was doubt? He had admitted he didn't know what love was about. He knew what seduction was about, though. This was seduction. This night of stars and wine and dining on the beach.

'Oh, Daniel,' she cried sorrowfully, her eyes filling with tears. How could he have done this to her? It was cruel.

Her eyes, widened by those trapped tears, could scarcely

focus on his face as she backed away from him. Her head was light and woozy and she wanted to run but her legs were heavy and the sand dragged at her bare feet so that it was more like a scramble for freedom than a dash for it.

He caught her at the water's edge, just as a ripple of warm water whooshed over her toes, sobering her completely. She had meant to run to the safety of the cottage but the night had disorientated her. He drew her back, back onto damp, warm sand. His eyes glinted angrily as he spun her round to face him.

'I said no escape, Karis. Face me, face us,' he growled.

'I am facing us,' Karis cried tears flooding her eyes. 'And not liking what I see. This is turning into a pantomime—a pantomime of seduction. The stars, the moon, and then...then the earth moving for us...and then...then what, Daniel? The cold reality of day. Disappointment, failure, guilt—all...all the horrible things that we both know so much about...'

She sobbed uncontrollably now and stepped back, stumbling in the ripples of sand. He reached for her and they fell together, sprawled on the shore. With a groan of despair Daniel held her tightly, trembling in his arms.

'My poor darling. Life has blinded you, Karis. You can't see any more. All this tonight was done from the heart, not to hurt you. Never that. Everything was done to please you. I want you in my life, Karis; can't you see that?'

His mouth sought hers, promising so much and confusing her reasoning. He wanted her in his life. And she wanted it more than anything she had ever desired. His kisses powered the last festering doubt from her mind. She clung to him, breathing his name when their lips parted, seeking them again when he slid his hands into her hair. She felt the weight of him against her, his power and his desire refusing to be denied. The sound of the sea rushed in her ears and the damp sand soaked into her dress but nothing mattered as desire flooded her.

His kisses covered her face and throat and shoulders. She arched against him, fire eating at her very soul. Dazed with passion, she was scarcely aware he was tearing her dress from her, his own shirt from his back. And then there was calm—a delicious calm that soothed her body and mind. His lips ran over her damp skin—over her breasts, down over the smooth planes of her stomach, her thighs. Then came the fire again—a need that had her crying out his name.

Soft, tantalising strokes of temptation passed over her thighs, sending her heart wild with desire. His arousal touched her and she shivered with pleasure and clung to him even more tightly, ravaging his throat with kisses of fire. He pressed into her and she flowered for him and he groaned passionately and thrust further, deeper into her, claiming her in a ritual of rhythm that trapped her breath in her throat.

Overwhelmed with desire, she matched his every movement of thrusting passion, only aware of her love firing her, of the need to please him and forever claim him as her own. And then came sweet pleasure as the ache inside her built to an overpowering desire to let go. He knew and held her suspended in time, prolonging her pleasure, enhancing it till she thrashed wildly under him, crying out for release.

It flooded them as the swell of the sea rose with them, carrying them to some mysterious far-off world where fire soothed, where senses spun, where dreams were promised and fulfilled. Sensation after delicious sensation thrummed through their bodies as, exhausted, they lay in each other's arms, the warm, frothy water lapping around them, balming their skin.

He lifted her then, effortlessly, as if she were weightless, and kissing her wet lips, he deposited her on dry sand. Wordlessly he moved back to the water's edge and rescued their discarded clothes and she watched in awe as, silhouetted against a silver sea, he came back to her, his body so powerful and sleek like some beautiful mythical god stepping out from the depths of the sea.

Neither spoke as he flung the bundle of sopping wet clothes on the dry shore and then took her in his arms, both naked, both uncaring because there was no one to witness them but the moon. His kiss was as full of promise as his lovemaking had been, a promise not to hurt her but to cherish her for evermore.

Back at the cottage Daniel showered them both and they laughed softly. Still dazed by the depth of their union, neither uttered a word. Karis let him dry her and lead her to her bedroom. From a distance the faint rhythmic thrum of a steel band at the party melded with the croak of tree frogs in the hot Caribbean night air but Karis wouldn't allow the sounds to encroach the euphoria of the night. The outside world didn't exist, not yet.

They lay together on the bed and Daniel took her in his arms and made love to her again and again. They were insatiable together, wanting and wanting till exhaustion overcame them and their strength was spent, leaving them sated and languorous, sleep claiming them at last.

Karis awoke, instinctively knowing it was late. There were sounds, ones she wasn't familiar with because she was always the first to rise and tend to the children.

The children! Guilt spurred her up from the bed. Saffron had said she would bed the children down at her sister's if the party ran too late. If they showed any signs of objecting she would bring them back to the cottage. Why hadn't she considered that last night? Saffron could have brought the children back to the cottage and found her and Daniel...

She sat on the edge of the bed and held her head in her

hands. She felt shame and guilt and just about every other negative emotion flood punishingly through her.

He'd bewitched her. Daniel Kennedy had bewitched her, cast some spurious spell over her, making her feel free and wanted and loved, and she'd given no thought to her responsibilities.

'Oh, God,' she moaned, a delicious ache swamping her as she got to her feet, a reminder of the most wonderful night of her life. But the day, the cold light of day...except it wasn't cold, it was heavy with a cloying heat.

'Oh, Daniel,' she breathed happily as she noticed a small glass vase of hibiscus flowers and jasmine at her bedside. There was no sign of him but he had left his mark—a beautifully fragrant start to the day. Karis lowered her mouth to the cool blooms and kissed them lightly.

Josh leapt on her as she joined Saffron and the children for breakfast on the verandah as usual.

'I danced all night, Kari. Tara too; she fell over a lot but she didn't cry, just laughed. Then we slept, all in a big bed with Didi and Marcus.'

'We had such a good time.' Saffron laughed, pouring coffee for Karis as she hugged Josh.

Sleepily Tara tottered to Karis and she pulled her up into her arms. Josh shifted to make room for her, bubbling over with excitement, telling her all about the singing and dancing and the games they had played.

Karis thought she had never been happier but at the same time she felt an enormous dragging weight around her heart. Was it possible to be happy and desperate in the same wash of emotion?

'Where's Daniel?' Karis asked Saffron when Josh had calmed down and led Tara away to their bedrooms to play.

Saffron shrugged. 'Said something about having to do what a man's gotta do.'

Karis smiled secretly. Obviously clearing up the beach after last night. She sat back and drank her coffee. Their clothes, freshly washed, waved in the breeze on the line from the verandah to a tree in the garden and the sight of them flushed Karis's heart with happiness.

'That dress, you ruined it swimming in it last night. Silk don't like salt water,' Saffron told her disapprovingly as she busied herself clearing the breakfast things from the table. 'And that Fiesta, she ain't gonna be happy her best chairs was out all night on the beach, nor her best silver and crystal.'

She paused and in that pause Karis shifted uncomfortably, unable to meet her gaze. Saffron was cross with them, worried in case it came back on her if Fiesta found out. The mention of the dress had sounded censorious, as if it was all right to hint at love but to act on it was a crime. Saffron's mood acted on Karis's emotions immediately, bringing them crashing down. They had been irresponsible last night, in so many ways. Yes, it was the cold light of day and it wasn't a nice feeling at all.

'But I guess she need never know,' Saffron added, and then, hands on hips, she started to laugh, a low, infectious laugh that rocked her body to and fro.

In relief Karis laughed with her. 'Saffron, you are incorrigible,' she stated as she ran barefoot down the verandah steps.

She slowed her pace as she went through the gardens towards the beach. Ferns and lush drooping hibiscus flowers brushed at her thin cotton skirt and a tiny hummingbird narrowly missed her tousled hair but Karis couldn't fully appreciate the beauty of it all. The prospect of facing Daniel this morning filled her with foreboding but it was best to get it over with without the children around. After last night there should be no doubt but...but there was, just a small creeping doubt that it might not be the same this morning.

She stood back from the beach, hidden behind oleander, and

watched him. Barefoot and in shorts, no shirt, he was piling the silver and china into a box. His features looked set and her heart pulsed nervously. Was he regretting it all, inwardly chastising himself for allowing the magic of the night to run away with them?

Boldly she stepped forward and Daniel's head came up and he gave her such a warm smile that she felt the doubt slide away from her.

'Clearing up the scene of the crime,' he told her with a wide grin.

Karis stopped where she was, her blood running cold, her heart crashing in her chest. A crime. She had thought the same in connection with Saffron's attitude. It had been a crime—exactly what sort she couldn't begin to analyse, but it had been wrong all the same, something they should never have allowed to happen.

'You should have heard Saffron this morning, wailing that Fiesta would go crazy if she found out. She made me feel like a criminal... Karis, darling, what's wrong?'

Suddenly he was there, holding her shoulders, so tenderly, so lovingly.

'Karis,' he whispered with concern. 'What is it?'

She couldn't answer. Her throat was dry, her heartbeat irregular, her very bones crumbling.

He pulled her into his arms and let out a groan. 'I know, I know,' he murmured into her hair.

'You don't,' she uttered weakly against him. 'Oh, Daniel, what have we done? I mean, it was wrong and now—'

'Don't say you regret it.'

He pushed her back from him to look down into her pinched face. 'Listen, darling, I don't regret it, not any of it. It was what we both wanted.' He lifted her downturned chin and looked deep into her eyes. 'Talk about it, sweetheart. I want to know what is troubling you.'

She knew then that she couldn't tell him anything about this pain she felt deep inside, this fear that she might be hurt again. The guilt she hadn't given a thought to last night when she was allowing herself to be bewitched by him. She had succumbed to temptation, had allowed all thoughts of Simone to be spiralled away on a whirlwind of desire. She'd believed that his relationship with Simone was an arrangement easily dealt with but hadn't she been just too gullible? They had come here together and Simone was still here, out on a fishing trip but nevertheless still involved.

She smiled through the mist of tears she was trying not to let betray her. She took a deep breath.

'It...it's a woman's thing, Daniel,' she breathed. 'Insecurity and all that. I awoke this morning and wanted you to be there because that would make it easier, you know, lying together in bed. I got up and the children—'

'You feel guilty because of the children?'

Yes, that was it—not all of it but it would do.

'Yes,' she admitted quietly.

He laughed softly and held her close again and squeezed her eyes shut and breathed the delicious warm fragrance of his skin, the side of her face pressed to his chest.

'Silly girl, they are both too young to know what is going on. Last night was beautiful and nothing has changed this morning. It's all as it was so you have no need to be afraid. No insecurity, Karis.' He lifted her head and pressed a warm, adoring kiss to her lips and she clung to him till he eased her back from him. 'Now, sweetheart, are you going to let me clear all this evidence or would you rather see me suffer the wrath of Saffron?'

With a smile Karis teased, 'I wouldn't wish that on my worst enemy. I have to get back to the cottage anyway.'

'See you later,' he murmured, and kissed her forehead before she turned away.

No, nothing had changed since last night, Karis thought, her heart tearing painfully. The children, Simone, they were nothing to what was really bothering her. It was all as it had been last night. He hadn't said he loved her then and he hadn't said it just now and she knew that was troubling her more than anything else in the world.

CHAPTER EIGHT

EUPHORIC days passed in which Karis urged unwanted thoughts from her head, sometimes quite successfully. It was easy to keep her emotions at bay during the days because of the presence of the children. The nights gave Karis the heartache but were tempered with joy too.

Once the children were in bed, both sleeping soundly because of spent energy, the time was hers and Daniel's. There was supper on the verandah watching fireflies, talking about Josh's progress, which was going from good to better; even Tara's new teeth were discussed, as if...as if they were a family. Then later Daniel would take her in his arms and they would make love and always but always Karis would wake in her bed alone. It was never questioned, just accepted by them both that it was necessary for the children, and Saffron, of course.

'Just us, Josh. No one else, I promise you.'

'What's going on?' Karis asked as she stepped into the kitchen.

Daniel looked up at her and smiled. He and Josh were having breakfast, Saffron had fed Tara and was clearing up the debris and Tara was playing out on the verandah.

'I've just suggested a boat trip, not a fishing trip with other people, just the four of us.'

'To that island Saffron just told you about?' Josh quizzed, nearly convinced it was a good idea.

'What island?' Karis asked, leaning across them for the coffee-pot.

'San Pierre,' Saffron told her, though the question hadn't

been directed at her. 'A little island east of here. No one there. You can stay over. There's an old hut there the fishermen use if the weather cuts up rough, but they won't be there now and...'

Talk of fishermen and fishing trips alerted Karis to the fact that today was when Fiesta's fishing cruise was due back. And with its return would come a certain Simone who undoubtedly would want to see Daniel and if they were away on a trip of their own he wouldn't be here.

Karis sank into a chair and poured coffee for herself, her heart thudding painfully. Daniel had suggested his trip with that in mind, obviously. So he had a guilty conscience after all. He couldn't face her and when Karis came to think of it she didn't think she could face her either. Simone was one of the unwanted thoughts she'd managed to banish from her mind these past few wonderful days, and now it crowded her head with cloying possession.

'What do you say, then, Karis? It would be great fun,' Daniel said.

'Yeah,' Josh shouted, warming to the idea. 'It'll be an adventure. We can pretend we're pirates and—'

'No!' Karis said quickly, and suddenly all eyes were on her.

She felt herself go hot all over, 'I mean, well, it might be dangerous,' she amended.

Saffron laughed. 'There ain't danger on a deserted island with—'

'OK, Saffron, that's enough,' Daniel interrupted. He was still watching Karis, frowning slightly. 'You have duties, don't you?'

Karis flushed and got to her feet. 'Yes, of course,' she muttered, and started to clear the table.

'I'm talking to Saffron,' Daniel snapped, glaring at Karis now as if she had gone crazy.

'Saints alive,' Saffron huffed, and went out to the verandah, gathering Tara up into her arms and padding off towards the bedrooms.

Josh, missing the sudden tension which had crowded the room, rushed out of the kitchen after her, excitedly saying he was going to pack for the adventure.

'Now see what you've done,' Karis challenged before Daniel could speak. Attack was the best form of defence. She knew it was in his mind to attack her for objecting to his stupid idea. She stacked dirty dishes and gabbled on. 'You've upset Saffron by snapping at her and hyped Josh up into a frenzy of excitement and the idea of going off to an island we know nothing about is ridiculous.'

'You are being ridiculous, Karis,' he said calmly. 'Now tell me, what's the real objection to going?'

'What do you mean, "what's the real objection"?' she flamed, crashing the dishes into the sink.

He was behind her in a flash and before she knew it she was thrust back in her chair with him glaring at her from across the table. He leaned forward and poured her more coffee. He looked angry but he was controlling it.

'It certainly hasn't anything to do with uninhabited islands,' he challenged. 'What are you expecting—marauding Indians, dinosaurs, creatures from the deep? The island is safe. Saffron wouldn't have—'

'Is this her idea?' Karis questioned brittly. What was she up to now?

'No, my idea,' he grated back at her. 'I thought we'd get off this island for a few days. Things are going well with Josh and he's ready for it.'

'Huh! He didn't sound ready for it when I came in just now. You were promising—'

'He got the wrong end of the stick when I suggested it, thought it was another fishing trip. I was reassuring him, that was all. You saw for yourself he was enthusiastic about it when he realised it was a trip for just us. It will do us all good to get off this island and—'

'Bored already?' she interjected sarcastically.

She'd known it wouldn't last—this idyllic existence. Daniel was restless for more reasons than she suspected. He wanted to avoid facing Simone today and was looking for escape from this domestic routine they had slipped into. What a fool she had been to think he cared. He didn't; he only wanted her for the time he was here, to ease the way for him with his son. Now he was probably thinking time away from his business was costing him and he was restless. Softly, softly, he'd said once. An adventure on another island and then the next step would be taking Josh to St Lucia and the step after that a flight back to the States. Softly, softly. Out of her life. Both of them gone for ever. She was numb with cold realisation.

'No, I am not bored,' he told her levelly, but there was an underlying anger to the words. 'And I don't like the suggestion that you think I am. What's this all about, Karis? There's more to it than meets the eye. Why the sudden objection to a trip that will be a lot of fun for us all?'

Karis met his eyes. Her throat felt so tight. She was vulnerable again, her insecurity bubbling like a poison inside her. It was the day that had brought it on; why *this* day to leave the island, the day Simone would be returning from the fishing trip? Why not tomorrow, after he had seen her and told her about their affair? Because he would tell her; because they had a past together, he would tell her. Her blood suddenly ran cold. *Wouldn't he?*

Shakily she got up from the table and went outside, hot air engulfing her in contrast to the cool air-conditioning of the kitchen. She needed to think. Question why she had been such a fool in believing it was over between him and Simone. It hadn't been mentioned since. She had grasped at a hint, that was all, known nothing for sure.

He swung her round to face him as she gripped the rail of the verandah, needing its strength to keep her on her feet. His grey eyes were dark and menacing, narrowed and not understanding.

'What's got into you?' he ground out.

She met his eyes bravely. He had no right to be angry with her when he was at fault for not being honest with her and not being honest with Simone. It wasn't over with her yet; if it was he would be staying to stand his ground. He didn't want to face Simone yet because he wasn't sure. Whether he liked it or not he was going to have to make a choice because he couldn't have both of them. By getting away from the island he would have time to think. Well, she wasn't going to give him the time. She was going to make the choice for him very simple.

'I don't want to go on this trip with you, Daniel,' she said softly but firmly. And then she couldn't meet his gaze any longer. He would see her pain and she had to come out of this with some pride if nothing else. She lowered her eyes. 'I...I've had enough, you see. I don't see the point in going on the way we are...' She heard him take a sharp breath and rushed on. 'Josh is doing well and that is what we set out to accomplish and—'

He gripped her chin suddenly, jerked her face up so she was forced to look at him. His eyes were dark and furious, his jawline set hard with tension.

'Are you saying you've been the way you've been with me for Josh's sake?' he growled angrily.

She couldn't speak. Love had powered her, and not love for Josh but love for him. Josh had nothing to do with it but to admit that would be to crumble the very last of her pride.

'Answer me,' he ordered roughly, jerking her chin.

She twisted her face from him but his hands went to her

shoulders again, preventing her escape before he got an answer. She gave him one.

'There doesn't have to be a reason, Daniel,' she seethed at last. 'Things happen, things end. Why should you care? You have Josh now, healed and repaired. It's what you came for. What happened between us is incidental. Simone is back today and I'm glad because it gets me off the hook. You can take up with her where you left off because it really doesn't matter to me.'

He let her go as if suddenly she were a deadly virus he didn't want to infect himself with. His eyes narrowed with fury. Somehow his anger strengthened her. A long while back in her life she had vowed never to be weak again. Aiden had taught her so much, after his death. Not to be used, not to be blind to reality, not to trust so easily. And yet she had done it again, allowed herself to be moonstruck, weakened and blinded by her love for Daniel. This time it was a thousand times worse, though, because her deep, deep love for Daniel was bigger, stronger, painfully more powerful than any feelings she'd ever had for Aiden. Then she had been young and naive; now...now she had no excuses. She'd learnt nothing and that realisation angered her.

'And don't look at me as if I'm beneath you,' she raged, because she couldn't think of anything else to say.

He shook his head in disbelief. 'Oh, you are, sweetheart, way beneath me, down there in the pit of contempt. Tossing me back to Simone, are you?'

'Where you belong...where...where your guilty conscience should be troubling you,' she whispered hoarsely.

'Guilty conscience?' he repeated darkly. 'The only guilt I ever suffered was after my wife died and with good reason and I've coped with it. I certainly don't have a conscience over Simone.'

'Well, you should have! After the way you have treated her,

behind her back with me, you damned well should have a conscience!'

'Well, I don't!' He snatched at her wrist and brought it up between them as if he was going to strike her with her own hand. His voice was furious as he growled at her, 'My conscience is clear over Simone because we talked about our problems before she went on her fishing trip. We both knew it wasn't working, for her because Josh couldn't take to her, for me because of you...' A gasp broke in Karis's throat.

'She'd already seen that for herself anyway,' Daniel went on, eyes glittering. 'She knew me well enough to know that from the very first day here you got under my skin. Simone and I parted amicably before I made love to you so don't talk to me about consciences. Mine is clear.'

Karis thought that was it, that he would let her go and storm off, but he had something more to stab at her. 'You know, Simone understood that it wouldn't work for us but one thing she couldn't grasp. She laughed in my face when I told her about you and how I felt about you. She said I was a bloody fool. And do you know something?' His grip tightened painfully for a brief second and then he tossed her wrist back at her with contempt, eyes black with fury. 'She was bloody right!'

Karis stood for a very long time on the verandah after he stormed off towards the plantation house. Rigid with shock, she gripped the rail till her fingers went white. Her heart was cold and dead inside her, lifeless because it didn't deserve to beat. What had she done? What had she spoiled? It was all ruined, poisoned, scarred. He *did* care and she had flung it back in his face because of her own stupid insecurity. She couldn't even apportion blame to Aiden any more. This was her doing, only hers, and there were no excuses, none but one. Not vulnerability or gullibility, just plain old stupidity for not having faith in him.

'Saffron is going to pack a huge hamper for us and I'm taking my spade so we can dig for treasure.'

Blindly Karis stared down at Josh. He usually ran along the wooden deck of the verandah like a herd of elephants. This time she had been grovelling so deep in that pit of contempt Daniel had thrown her in that she hadn't heard him coming. He looked up at her, his face glowing with happiness and excitement.

'Come on,' he demanded impatiently, tugging at her shorts. 'You have to pack things too.'

'I think it best you leave Tara behind with me,' Saffron said as she came out of the bedroom further along the verandah with Tara clinging to her. 'She won't like digging for treasure. It will do you grown-ups good to be on your own.'

'I'm not a grown-up,' Josh laughed.

'You very nearly are, child,' Saffron retorted, also laughing, sweeping into the kitchen.

Karis had heard and watched it all in a daze. There wasn't going to be a trip. They couldn't go now. It was impossible. How could she tell him, little Josh, that they couldn't go? That she had spoilt everything because of her own stupidity?

'Saffron is going to cook us rotis to take and I'm going to help,' Josh cried, and ran into the kitchen behind them.

Numbly Karis fled to her bedroom and flung herself down on the bed. The bed they had loved in...but he'd never said and because of that small, silly, silly omission she had ruined it all. He did care, had cared deeply enough to finish with Simone before giving himself to her. And he had given oh, so much. He had confided in her and done that crazy romantic barbecue on the beach, had loved her till dawn, only creeping away from her bed because of his son's feelings and the necessity for propriety with Saffron.

Saffron knew; she had always known; she had seen it in the

way he had looked at her. And she hadn't believed her, because of Simone and her past, Aiden and...and everything.

'Get up, Karis.'

Karis shot up from the bed, her head reeling. Had she slept? Impossible. She'd never sleep again. Her eyes widened at the sight of Daniel towering over her. Saffron was the one who was blind. There was no love in his eyes. They were as unreadable as they had been the day he had arrived.

'Get yourself together. Josh is impatient to get going.' His tone was clipped and authoritative, that of one who paid the wages.

'I'm not going...' she began, smoothing her crumpled shorts.

'You're coming, because I've come too far with my son to risk you ruining it now.'

'It will ruin it if I come!' she protested. Couldn't he see that?

His eyes flashed anger at her. 'Swallow your dislike of me long enough to do this for the boy,' he said thickly. 'It shouldn't be too hard for you. You're adept at fooling people.'

He believed she didn't like him; after all they had been to each other he believed she didn't care. It hurt so badly it was a physical pain deep inside her. And yet she hadn't had faith in him either, hadn't believed that he truly cared for her and not Simone. Always the doubt, never the certainty. This was what Aiden had done to her; he had undermined her that terrible night he had shown his uncaring attitude to her joyful news that they were going to have a baby. She shuddered inside. She was doing it again—blaming someone else for her own inadequacies. She mustn't, not ever again.

'Go on your own with Josh,' she suggested quickly. It would be impossible for her to go; the tension between them would be unbearable. 'He's your son and—'

'And you are still his carer,' he insisted angrily. 'And until I terminate the arrangement that's what you are going to be.'

Until he decided to take Josh away, she thought despairingly. And that would be soon now because she had smoothed the path for them both and she was expendable. The agony of the thought drove her on.

'So I'm the hired help again, am I? Or perhaps I always was!' she hissed at him.

'You said that, not me,' he breathed heavily. 'And you had the nerve to question my conscience. Where was yours when—?'

A small noise at the door had them both swinging round. Josh stood in the doorway, his face contorted with fear, his slight body as tense as whipcord. His mouth was moving, trying to form words.

Karis froze, her heart breaking inside her. What had he heard? She dared not look at Daniel, who was standing next to her. She could feel his tension, though, the heat of his body fired by the shock of Josh's appearance and the inability of the frightened little boy to speak. Oh, no, all their good work gone to waste and it was all her fault.

'Women!' Daniel laughed suddenly. 'Honestly, Josh, what are we going to do with her? Karis can't decide what to bring on the adventure. I expect she'll bring the kitchen sink in the end.'

Oh, it was feeble, but a start. She helped by laughing in protest. 'Well, I've never been on an adventure before so what do you expect? What will I need now?'

Blindly she lurched towards the wardrobe and flung it open and snatched at T-shirts and shorts, her hands shaking with panic. Josh wasn't responding. From the corner of her eye she could see he hadn't moved. He was still frozen to the spot, confused, disorientated because of what he had seen and overheard, her and Daniel practically at each other's throats. Oh, God, they had failed him, failed him miserably.

'Not these, I think,' Daniel laughed, picking up a pair of strappy high heels and holding them up for Josh to see. Karis had brought them with her from England and never worn them. 'Pirates don't wear high heels, do they, Josh?'

'Th-th...'

Oh, no. Josh's face was flushed and he was struggling to form the words on his lips. Karis couldn't bear it; her heart tore painfully.

'They...they wear earrings,' he blurted suddenly.

Daniel laughed out loud and a tentative smile hovered on Josh's small mouth.

'There you are, Karis. It's a start. You'd better pack your earrings or you won't be allowed to come.'

'Josh!' Saffron called from the verandah. 'Leroy's brought the boat.'

'The boat's here!' Josh cried, fully recovered now. 'Come on, hurry.' He tore off along the verandah, whooping with excitement.

Karis closed her eyes, desperately trying to regulate her tempestuous heartbeat. It was all right. It was going to be all right. Relief washed over her like spring rain, calming her, soothing her, bringing her down and down. She opened her eyes and then knew it could never be right. Daniel was staring at her hard, his eyes shards of anger—anger he had so skilfully hidden from his son. But not from her. She got the full icy blast of it.

'Let that be a lesson to you,' he rasped bitterly. 'Don't you ever do that to my son again. You swallow every emotion but love for Josh on this trip or your life won't be worth living.' With that he turned and walked stiffly out of her bedroom.

And I might as well walk the plank now and get it over with, Karis thought achingly, her eyes burning with grief.

There was no escape. She had to go with them, for Josh's sake, not Daniel's because he really didn't care a damn for her, only Josh, only his precious son. And that was what it had been about from the start, she realised with an aching sense of loss. For the love of Josh. Numbly Karis started to push clothes into a holdall.

Josh was first ashore, scrambling over the side of the small covered fishing boat Daniel had borrowed from Leroy's brother to a small wooden jetty jutting out from the beach. He tied up as his father instructed while Daniel cut the engine. Karis noted Josh's hands were shaking with excitement.

'Hold on, Josh,' she shouted as he was about to leap off the side of the jetty to explore the tiny island. 'There might be dragons lurking around,' she teased.

'Do you want to scare the life out of him?' Daniel hissed under his breath at her as he threw their bags onto the jetty.

'Dragons live in caves, not on tropical islands.' Josh giggled, jumping up and down with impatience. 'Come on, hurry up.'

Karis afforded Daniel a small smile. She still knew Josh better than he did but she didn't want to rub it in.

'OK, so what do I know?' he muttered under his breath again, getting her message anyway.

Subliminal thoughts. He'd just read her as he had read her before, seeing something she was hardly aware of herself. Could she put it to good use? Subliminally show him she was sorry, she was in love with him and insecurity had made her say crazy things this morning? She sighed. She wasn't that clever.

'What was the sigh for? Wishing you weren't here?' he suggested cruelly.

She couldn't respond, not the way he expected. 'It's beautiful,' she murmured, shading her eyes against the glare of the sun on white, white sands. 'Sigh-inducing beautiful,' she added.

He laughed but she wasn't sure if it was a mocking laugh or not.

'Come on!' Josh urged impatiently.

They walked the plank together, the three of them, Josh skipping between them till they reached the end of the rickety jetty where he leaped off into deep fine white sand.

'It is beautiful,' Daniel agreed as he reached out to help Karis down.

She remembered him taking Simone's elbow on the jetty on Levos that first day. The thought tugged painfully at her and she took a deep breath to rid herself of it.

'Another sigh?'

Karis turned on him angrily. 'Can't I breathe without you commenting sarcastically?'

'Keep your voice down!' he bit out. He strode on ahead of her, breaking into a run to catch Josh up before he burst into the old bleached wooden hut on stilts at the edge of the beach.

No, I won't, she thought recklessly, and then shouted at the top of her voice, 'Watch out for dragons and ten-legged monsters in there! And I don't mean the mythical sort!'

'What does mythical mean?' Josh asked his father as he slipped his hand into his, suddenly nervous at the closed door in front of them.

'Just your moth...just Karis trying to be funny,' Daniel said sardonically.

Karis heard. She was right behind them, on the last step. She heard and heat flooded her fiercely. Daniel had nearly said 'mother'; he had corrected himself in time for Josh but not for Karis. Daniel turned and obviously knew she'd heard because colour suffused his throat. Their eyes locked, only for a brief, painful second, but long enough for Karis to know that he hadn't made the mistake because he was thinking of his wife.

She didn't know how she knew; she just did. Hope sprang inside her—a tiny, tiny nub of hope.

'Cowards!' she taunted, recovering quickly. She stepped around them both, kicked the door back with her bare foot and stepped inside, only to freeze, throw up her hands and let out a blood-curdling scream.

Josh threw himself at her, shrieking at the top of his voice and then laughing hysterically. Karis swept him up into her arms and spun him around and Josh clung to her, laughing till his face was red. Karis stopped and let Josh down. Daniel stood frozen in the doorway, clutching his chest with both hands.

'Christ, the pair of you frightened the life out of me,' he said nervously.

'We always do that,' Josh told him breathlessly. 'We call it spooky time. Kari pretends to be a monster and we scream. Saffron says you mustn't use that word unless you are praying or in church; otherwise it's a swear word. I'm going to bring the stuff in.' He rushed out and leapt down all the steps at once and went haring down the beach to where they had left the bags.

'Since when has "spooky" been a swear word?' Daniel asked in mock innocence.

Karis's heart squeezed as a broad grin spread across his face. She smiled to match his, a warm glow spreading inside her. But softly, softly, she warned herself.

'Let that be a warning to you,' she told him, mischief sparkling in her eyes. 'If you want to swear, go behind a palm tree to do it...or the monsters will get you,' she added in a scary voice as she swept past him to catch Josh up.

An hour later they had unpacked, circled the island twice—it really was very small—and gathered driftwood for a fire later.

'This is my bed,' Josh claimed, leaping onto the bunk under the reeded window at the end of the one room.

There were four crude bunks in the hut, all with mattresses stuffed with dry palm leaves. Saffron had packed thin cotton blankets for them and Josh had laid one on each bed, leaving the fourth stacked with their clothes and towels and the rest of the stuff they had brought. He knelt up on his bed and propped open the woven reed flap. 'It's so hot.'

Because of the smallness and the flatness of the island a cooling breeze had earlier had Daniel commenting that it was refreshing not to have humidity pressing down on them all the time.

'Well, if you will rush around at breakneck speed all the time, is it any wonder you are hot?' Daniel told him, searching in a box for candles for later.

'I'm a boy. Boys rush around,' Josh told him knowledgeably, and Karis and Daniel laughed.

When it was dark they lit the fire outside and Daniel warmed Saffron's rotis on a griddle they'd found in a box in the hut. The spicy pastries were as good cold as they were hot but Daniel insisted that pirates didn't eat cold food, and besides, the fire was a warning to other pirates that this island was already occupied and whomsoever set foot on it would fear for their lives.

Later Josh lay on his bed, exhausted, eyelids drooping, and Daniel told him the story of Henry Morgan who rode the high seas, the most daring and successful pirate in the Caribbean, and who eventually won respect and was knighted by King Charles the Second in England and returned to Jamaica to become Governor.

'Was he Fiesta's father?' Josh murmured faintly, but was asleep before Daniel could think of an answer to that.

'Was he?' Karis asked, feigning seriousness, when Daniel joined her outside on the top set of the stilted hut.

Daniel sat beside her, barefoot as she was. He didn't touch her and she hadn't expected him to. After only a few hours on this scrap of pure paradise they had all relaxed immeasurably. But not relaxed enough for Daniel to take her in his arms and for Karis to murmur her apologies and tell him she hadn't meant what she had said and she loved him and had only been spurred by jealousy and insecurity and all things mad and bad. Maybe tomorrow, or the day after, but certainly before they left here. They couldn't return to Levos the way they had left it, angry and hurt with each other.

'He was a womaniser, you know.'

'Who, Fiesta's father?' Karis teased.

'Henry Morgan, idiot,' he laughed.

Karis took 'idiot' as a term of endearment.

'He plied one lovely lady with gifts—silver, crystal and fine china; all that he plundered, he offered her.'

Karis smiled secretly into the dark warm night. Like somebody else, she recalled, remembering the wondrous beach barbecue under the stars with Fiesta's treasures.

'All in vain. She spurned him,' he went on quietly. 'Said she'd rather die than suffer dishonour at his hands.'

'First of the feminists,' Karis murmured under her breath. 'So did the bold pirate win the fair maiden in the end?'

He reached out and took her hand and squeezed it gently. His voice was low and filled with humour as he said, 'No. He was so mad he locked her up in a room without a stitch of clothing on her back.'

Karis was still smiling when, still in shorts and T-shirt, she slid under the thin cotton blanket and lay on her back in the bed next to Josh's. She stared up at the stars through a hole in the palm-leaf roof, the same stars that Daniel had traded his soul with the gods for.

He was outside now, dousing the last embers of the fire, under those stars.

She'd trade her soul to those same gods. Not for the stars, though, but for Daniel to forgive, for Daniel to love her, for it all to be right in the morning or even the afternoon.

'Come on, Josh. Dig deeper. The map says Henry Morgan's treasure is buried here, where the shadows of two palm trees cross.'

Josh sat back on his heels, flushed with effort, beads of perspiration breaking out on his brow. 'I'm tired and the sun keeps moving the cross. Just now it was over there.'

Karis grinned at Daniel and gave him a look that said, You've been caught out.

'Yes, but it's the three o'clock sun, just here. Let's dig a bit deeper.' With Josh's spade and the old griddle pan they worked feverishly till Josh let out a yelp of excitement.

'I've found it!'

He pulled the old box out from the sand and opened it. Karis and Daniel sat grinning at him. Karis was in on the secret. While Josh had slept late that morning she had found Daniel digging on the beach. The day before he had noted the time of day two leaning palms had cast a shadowy cross on the sand and marked it with a stick. While he'd buried the box he'd brought with him, obviously having planned all this in Levos before they left, Karis had scratched out a rough map on a piece of flat driftwood that had escaped the fire the night before. They had placed it under the steps, sticking out so that Josh couldn't fail to see it.

'Shells and a book and a car...and a roti?' Josh cried. 'One of Saffron's rotis. How did that get in there?'

Karis shrugged. It had been her idea. Josh couldn't be allowed to think this was really Henry Morgan's treasure; not that he would—he wasn't anyone's fool—but just in case she had suggested the roti for fun.

'Oh, wow!' Josh exclaimed. In amongst the shells he'd found another box, a slim leather box.

Karis leaned forward. She hadn't seen that go in.

'Oh, a watch, a watch!' Josh cried, his fingers trembling as they scrambled to get the small gold child's watch out from the bands that held it in place. 'I've never had one. It's my first.'

Daniel strapped it to his wrist for him and asked, 'Can you tell the time?'

'Of course; Kari taught me.' He peered at the face. 'It's...' He hesitated. 'It's ten...no, quarter past two...no, ten past three.'

'Phew, that was close.' Daniel laughed and held Karis's eyes. 'I thought a dismissal might be on the cards,' he directed at her and she wasn't offended one bit.

'Something for Kari,' Josh declared as he picked up a small paper parcel with her name on it from the pile of shells left in the box. He thrust it at her.

Karis's eyes widened. She hadn't seen that go in either.

'Open it,' Josh urged.

Karis looked down at the small parcel and grinned. 'If this is another of Saffron's rotis... Oh.' Her heart stopped as she tore off the paper and unpeeled a layer of cotton wool.

'Oh, it's only an old ring,' Josh said with disappointment, and got up from the sand. 'I'm going to get a drink.'

Before turning away, he hesitated and then put his arms round Daniel's neck and squeezed him. The gesture took Karis and Daniel completely by surprise.

'Th-thank you for my watch. I...I'm going to wear it for ever.' He let go and, flushed with embarrassment, ran towards the hut.

Karis couldn't see for the film of tears that misted her eyes. She still held the ring in her hands as she knelt by the hole they had dug in the sand. But nothing mattered but what she had just witnessed—a loving son hugging his father.

'Karis?' Daniel murmured, bringing her out of her happy reverie.

'Oh, Daniel, you've made him so happy,' she breathed. 'Not just the gift; it was nothing to do with that. He hugged you.'

'I know,' Daniel said quietly, just a hint of a crack in his voice. 'Karis,' he urged. The tears in her eyes cleared and she saw him indicating the ring in her hand. 'It was my mother's. I've always carried it,' he told her tenderly. 'Sorry there's no box.'

Uncertainly Karis lowered her eyes and stared at the small ring nestling in the white cotton wool. It was exquisite, a tiny sapphire with tiny diamonds sparkling around it. Her eyes misted again, with tears of loss and grief she couldn't hold back. She bit her bottom lip, almost drawing blood in an effort for control.

'Th-thank you,' she murmured. Was this his parting gift to her? Her heart thudded desperately. He had what he had come for, his son back and with love and acceptance, and this was his thank-you for her help and now she wasn't wanted any more. She fought the tearing of her heart with all her might. 'It's...it's beautiful. Every...every time I wear it I'll...I'll think of...'

She scrambled to her feet, her legs hardly able to hold her up.

'Karis?'

Daniel came up with her, catching at her wrist to stop her rushing away. 'You'll think of what?' he demanded to know.

Her breath wouldn't come. She swallowed hard, inwardly praying the tears would stay at bay long enough for her to make her getaway. 'I'll...I'll think of you and...and Josh and...remember.'

The tears, hot and painful, spilled over. With a sob she

rushed away from him plunging the ring into the pocket of her shorts. There was nowhere to run to, no escape. Just the hut where Josh had fled to. She was on the top step before she had her despair under control. She had actually believed they had a chance, had allowed that small nub of hope to swell and pulse more certainly. But there was no hope, only a terrible loss that dragged painfully at her heart. Hastily she scrubbed the tears from her face with the palms of her hands and with her head held high she stepped inside with a smile because she couldn't let Josh see her distress.

'The treasure was a lovely surprise, wasn't it? Josh...?'

Josh was sprawled on the bed, flat out with exhaustion. Karis swallowed hard and stood by the bunk. She must hide her feelings from the boy. He must never know how she felt about his father. They were truly bonded now and once back in the States he would forget he'd ever had a nanny...perhaps they could keep in touch, though. A sob caught in her throat. No, they couldn't; it would be too painful.

'Oh, Josh,' she moaned softly, and leaned down and brushed the tousled hair from his brow.

Her heart contracted at the contact and nausea rushed up to her throat. She drew her hand back sharply as if she had been singed. The little boy was burning up.

'Josh,' she breathed worriedly, dropping to her knees and lifting his head from the bunk. 'Josh, darling, wake up, wake up,' she almost cried.

Josh groaned and flickered his eyes open and then closed them again, the effort too much for him.

White with shock and panic, Karis flew across the room. 'Daniel! Daniel!' she screamed frantically from the doorway.

CHAPTER NINE

'HE'S just overdone it,' Daniel said, crouching by the bunk and soothing his son's brow.

'It's more than that,' Karis insisted, wringing her hands with worry. She knew Josh, knew it was more. 'He's burning with a fever, Daniel, burning up.'

'You're right,' Daniel said with concern. 'Josh, how do you feel?' he asked softly.

Josh's eyes flickered open again, barely able to focus on his father's face. 'Where's Kari?' he murmured.

'Here, Josh, I'm here.' Karis dropped down to her knees beside Daniel and took the small boy's hot hand in hers.

'My head hurts,' he moaned.

'All right, Josh, it's all right,' Karis breathed soothingly.

Daniel and Karis stood up as Josh drifted off to sleep again. Outside Daniel raked his fingers through his hair. Karis was shaking with worry, her own brow furrowed and burning with concern.

'We have to get him back,' she told Daniel urgently.

He turned to her, distraught with worry. 'You think it's serious?' he breathed roughly.

'I...I don't know.' She rubbed her forehead, trying to think clearly. 'He was hot yesterday and this morning—'

'I made him dig...he said he was tired...he was tired yesterday—'

'It's not your fault, Daniel,' Karis said quickly. It was hers for not seeing the warning signs. Oh, God, she'd been so preoccupied with her feelings about Daniel it had clouded her reasoning on anything else. Josh was sick and she hadn't seen it.

'Let's go,' Daniel said brusquely. 'Leave all this. Get in the boat. I'll wrap him up and bring him down to the jetty.'

'What about going straight to St Lucia?' Karis suggested, panic grasping her ever tighter.

Daniel shook his head. 'Too far in an old fishing boat.'

'But there's no doctor on Levos,' Karis cried. 'Only Saffron's sister who makes up herbal remedies and—'

'Get in the boat, Karis,' Daniel ordered thickly and, white-faced, turned back into the hut.

Karis ran to the jetty where the boat was tied up as fast as her legs would carry her. Her fingers were numb and useless as she struggled with the worn rope.

Daniel came down the beach with his son in his arms and gently handed him to Karis before leaping in beside her to start the engine. Karis cradled the boy in her lap under the wattled shade of the old boat. Daniel was running the engine so fast she thought it would burn out before they got there. He swung the boat out to sea and the vibration and the swell made Josh sick and Karis knew he was seriously ill.

'Oh, hurry,' she murmured under her breath.

Her heart sank as an eternity later they were in sight of the jetty at Levos. The beach was crowded with Fiesta's guests, windsailing, drinking at the beach bar, laughing. How dared anyone laugh and have fun when Josh was so sick?

Daniel leapt out of the boat and tied up and then gathered his son protectively into his arms and started running along the jetty, his desperation showing as people stopped and stared, suddenly becoming aware of his urgency.

From then on to Karis it was all a blur. The next thing she knew they were inside the plantation house, Josh lying weak and fretful on a pink silk chaise longue in the cool, marble-floored reception hall, Daniel shouting to the guests who had swarmed inside, asking if there was a doctor amongst them.

'There's no doctor,' Fiesta said calmly. 'Now everybody out,' she ordered. 'This isn't a circus.' She slammed the huge front door of the house after them.

Daniel barked out orders to Fiesta then sat in a chair by the boy, holding his son's hand. Through a bank of fog Karis heard Fiesta asking for a helicopter over the phone, adding that it was urgent and a medical team was needed as well, and then Fiesta was grasping her arm and urging her to the back of the reception hall to the door that led through to the other rooms and the kitchens.

Karis's heart shredded. Fiesta wanted rid of her. Josh was in safe hands and she wasn't needed any more.

Fiesta swung her round at the door, holding her arms to steady her as she was shaking so hard. 'Karis, listen to me. Go out the back for quickness, to the cottage. Grab a bag of things for Daniel, Josh and yourself. You'll have to stay overnight in Castries at the very least. I know you'll want to make sure Tara is OK with Saffron but make it quick; the helicopter with a doctor and nurse is on it's way.'

'My...my things?' Karis gasped at her.

Fiesta smiled and gently squeezed her arms. 'Josh needs you and Daniel too. You are going to have to be strong for them both. Now get going.'

Karis flew like the wind.

She explained quickly to Saffron what had happened and Saffron only paused long enough to let out a wail of distress and then chant out some West Indian incantation before rushing around to pack for Karis. Karis stood by her daughter's cot, trying desperately to calm herself but up against too many odds. She couldn't stop shaking. Mercifully the dear child was sleeping and oblivious of all that was going on. She had a small smile of contentment curling her pink lips and Karis knew she was safe and silently blessed Saffron for being there for her.

'I hate leaving her, Saffron. The trip to the island was different. It was OK to leave her then but now...now everything is so...so desperate and—'

'That child knows me like she knows you,' Saffron chortled. 'Now you get going and bring that boy back safe and well. You tell him I'll have his favourite pumpkin pie waiting for him.'

Karis hugged her before speeding back to the plantation house with a bulging holdall.

Breathless, she scooted in the back way just as the drone of a helicopter approached. She stopped in horror in the doorway, ice-cold perspiration trickling down her back.

'I'll come with you, Daniel; you'll need me.'

Simone was standing stroking Daniel's arm as he gazed down at his son. 'We should have left earlier as I suggested, then none of this would have happened.'

Daniel let out a ragged sigh. 'You're right. I blame myself.'

Simone squeezed his arm lovingly. 'I knew you'd see reason. Forget all this nonsense now. We're going to be just fine.'

Numb with shock, Karis let the holdall slip to the floor. Simone was going with Daniel and Josh to the hospital and—

The front door burst open and Fiesta came in with a doctor and a nurse. Daniel stepped back from his son. There was talk, none of which Karis could take in because of the blood rushing in her head. People were suddenly milling around and Josh was being lifted. Karis stumbled forward, blindly, wanting to be with Josh...

'You're not needed now.'

Her arm was grasped to hold her back and suddenly she was facing the ice-cold gaze of Simone.

'You never were needed,' Simone whispered fiercely under

her breath. 'You were used, but you must have known that, a bright little thing like you.'

Karis's mouth dropped open in confusion. Josh was on a small stretcher, Daniel talking to the doctor, Fiesta with the nurse. They were going, leaving...

Simone smiled cruelly. 'But then perhaps you didn't,' she simpered. 'Let me put you straight now. Daniel used you as long as it took to win his son back. He has him now, and me, and don't you believe otherwise. You only have one thing to console yourself with: he doesn't blame you for Josh's illness, he blames himself for being such a fool.'

Blindly Karis backed off, shaking with shock and her insides balled with pain. She heard her name called by Daniel but it didn't register. It registered with Simone, though; she stiffened and swung round and suddenly Fiesta was at Simone's elbow, holding her back and pushing Karis forward with her other hand.

'Go, Karis,' Fiesta urged.

Karis stood by the window of the room next to Josh's. Tense and desperate, she waited for Daniel to come back. He'd acted like a man possessed on arrival at the hospital, rushing doctors into action, arranging for a room to be made available for them close to Josh. In the whirlwind of activity she had been surplus to requirements, standing back, drawing back from where she wasn't needed. She'd heard the word 'meningitis' whispered and had nearly fainted and then Daniel had wrapped his arm around her shoulders and guided her to this room where he had left her, urging her to rest till she was needed.

Rest? How could she rest? She'd paced the room a hundred times, refusing to think about what Simone had said as they'd left because Josh was more important. But when would she be needed? And who would need her? Daniel was coping well enough without her and Josh...Josh was in a coma—

'Daniel!' she sobbed, and flew across the room to him, flinging herself into his arms at the sight of his pale, drawn face.

He held her, smoothing her wild hair, murmuring to her softly, 'It's all right, darling, it's all right.'

'Oh, it's not. They...they said meningitis...'

He held her back from him, framed her pinched face in his hands. She saw him through a sea of desperate tears. Through his own despair he managed a small smile for her.

'We got him here in time,' he whispered. 'They've drawn off the spinal fluid to relieve the pressure on the brain—'

'Oh, no,' were the only words she could mouth before sliding down into a dark, warm pit.

Daniel was holding a paper cup of water to her lips when she came round. He was supporting her on the edge of the bed, holding her with one arm around her shoulders and the other urging her to drink.

'I...I'm supposed to be strong for you,' she uttered weakly after sipping the ice-cool water. 'And here I am, fainting all over the place.' She lifted her head, her eyes wide and distraught. 'I'm letting you down and I've let Josh down and—'

'You saved Josh's life, Karis,' he told her earnestly. 'It was you who said we had to get him back. I thought...I thought he'd just overdone it. If—'

'No, Daniel,' she pleaded. She knew what he was thinking and it didn't bear thinking about. 'How is he?'

'Sleeping. The doctor said he'll be drowsy for some time but he's going to be fine. It's a viral form, not so dangerous, and he's strong and—'

Karis's brain started working furiously, her heart pumping wildly. A virus! Tara! Tara had been all right when she'd left, sleeping peacefully, safe with Saffron, but... And the children at the party! Josh had slept with other children that night. She tried to get up from the edge of the bed, her head spinning. Daniel held onto her.

'Tara is all right,' he insisted, holding her and turning her to face him. 'When the doctor told me it was a virus I immediately called Levos. Fiesta assured me Tara is just fine and so are the rest of the children on the island. She had her suspicions about Josh's symptoms and checked on them all after we left. As an added precaution I've sent a doctor and nurse over to make sure, though Josh's doctor thinks Josh was just unlucky. He could have picked it up from the sea, swimming.'

'H-how did you know what I was thinking?' she said weakly, her whole body sagging with relief. He'd thought of everything: Tara, the other children on the island...

He smiled. 'Because, in case you haven't noticed, I'm a parent myself.'

'Oh, Daniel,' she breathed, 'you're a wonderful father.' His first thought after Josh had been her own daughter and then the children of the staff on the island. She was overwhelmed with love for him.

'And you're wonderful too,' he told her tenderly. 'Now, let's get ourselves sorted out.'

Gently he drew her up to her feet and smiled. 'Look at the pair of us—no shoes, still in shabby shorts and looking like a couple of pirates down on our luck. I think we'd better get ourselves freshened up before we see Josh.'

She nodded through her smiles and tears. She felt terrible and obviously looked it too and he looked no better.

'There's a shower room just there. I'll go and arrange some food—'

'Oh, I couldn't eat—'

'You must and you will. We are going to need your strength—'

Her head shot up. The crisis wasn't over yet and...

'Stop panicking,' Daniel told her reassuringly. 'Josh is going to be just fine. I wouldn't lie to you, Karis.' He bent and kissed her forehead lightly before leaving the room.

As he closed the door after him Karis let out a ragged sigh of exhaustion. He was right; they needed their strength to see Josh through this. The poor little boy would wake up in a strange hospital and want his...want his father at his side. It all rushed at her then and she went to the shower room because if she didn't flood herself with cool water she would flood herself with all the things she didn't want to think about.

But it was hopeless. As she kicked off her grubby shorts the little sapphire ring fell from the pocket, spun across the tiled floor and pinged against the wall tiles. In horror Karis gazed at it, words spinning through her head, Daniel's and Simone's, Simone's and Daniel's. He'd just said he wouldn't lie to her but he meant he wouldn't lie to her about Josh. Because he had deceived her, making her believe he cared, and then he had given the ring to her as a thank-you, a parting gift. She had seen him with Simone, reconciled, him agreeing with her that she was right and he was a fool.

In desperation Karis turned on the shower, stepped under the fierce jet and still it wouldn't go away—the nightmare of Simone's parting words. She had been used; she wasn't needed any more. Yet Daniel had called for her when they had been rushing for the helicopter—but no...only because he needed her some more, while Josh was sick. When he was better... She switched off the shower and stepped out.

'I managed to get some sandwiches and tea. Have you finished with the shower?'

Karis was combing out her wet hair by the window and jumped when he came back into the room with a tray.

'Yes,' she murmured.

'Feel better?' he asked before snatching a couple of towels from a pile on the bed.

'Much better,' she lied. How could she feel better when everything was so awful? Darling Josh so ill and her life in ruins once more. How could he worry about sandwiches and tea and whether the shower was free? Because he was trying to hide his deep concern for his son, she reasoned; because his son was his life and he would do anything for him.

And I must too, Karis vowed as she flung down her comb. I must be strong for Josh's sake and not think of myself.

She was sitting cross-legged on the bed sipping tea when he came out, tousling his hair with a towel, another knotted around his waist. She'd laid out fresh clothes for him on the other bed, light cotton trousers and a shirt, all newly laundered and without his smell, she knew, because she had pressed them to her face.

She couldn't look as he dressed, openly in front of her, as if they belonged to each other, man and wife, lovers, as once they had been. She didn't want her loss rubbed in, didn't want to see the wonderful body that had once been hers to love and to hold. It couldn't be so again, not ever.

'Mr and Mrs Kennedy, your son is asking for you,' a nurse said as she popped her head around the door.

Karis stared at her and then looked away in embarrassment. They thought they were married and Josh was their son. She gulped at her tea.

'Karis,' Daniel urged, and when she looked he was holding out his hand to her.

'H-he wants you,' she husked painfully.

'He's asking for his mummy and daddy,' the nurse told them with a smile.

Karis's heart squeezed tightly. The nurse was mistaken; he couldn't have said that; Josh had no mummy. Oh, no, he was delirious, drifting back in time, not knowing his mother was dead, wanting his mother so much and thinking she was still alive.

'Karis,' Daniel urged again, this time more insistently.

She stared blankly at Daniel. She was desperate to see the

boy but not like this, with him expecting his own mother to walk in. Fear gripped her and she couldn't move, not a muscle.

Daniel came across the room and snatched at her wrist. 'What's got into you?'

She couldn't answer but she made the effort for him. She went with Daniel, numb with grief, legs moving without conscious motivation, Daniel clutching at her wrist to steady her.

'Daddy.' Josh smiled weakly from the bed, as pale as the sheet he was lying on.

Karis froze in the doorway of the cool, dimly lit room, her senses reeling with a mixture of joy for Daniel and sorrow for herself. It was the very first time she had heard the boy call his father 'Daddy'. Daniel went to the bedside and took his son's hand in his.

'I'm here, son,' Karis heard him say in a low voice thick with love and relief.

Suddenly Daniel looked across at Karis and she saw his eyes were filled with tears and her own welled in happiness for him.

'Where's Mummy?' Josh whispered.

'She's here, Josh,' Daniel told him softly. 'Right by the door.'

A gasp caught in Karis's throat. Oh, he was wrong, so very wrong in doing this. This wasn't fair to Josh and it wasn't fair to her. She had to get out but she couldn't move. She seemed paralysed in some awful nightmare.

'I can't see her. Kari, I want you,' Josh moaned.

Karis hesitated, her head whirling. Then she moved forward slowly. Josh knew. The little boy knew the difference. She wasn't his mother but in his confused state perhaps he thought of her as his own. Suddenly she was at the other side of the bed and Josh was reaching for her hand and she took it and he clung to the two of them. His father one side of him, his...Karis the other.

'Where's my sister?' he asked.

'Tara's with Saffron,' Daniel said quickly. 'They are both waiting for you to get better, Josh. We'll be going back soon, very soon.'

'I want to go now...' he murmured, and then he drifted into sleep again.

'Leave him now,' the nurse said from behind them. 'He needs to sleep. You'll see a remarkable difference in him in the morning.'

In a daze Karis left the room and stood in the corridor, leaning against a cool wall and taking deep breaths to calm herself. It was night-time, she realised, glancing towards the window; it was pitch-dark outside. Time had stopped; the world outside went on, but her life had stopped. Daniel was still in Josh's room, talking to the nurse in soft whispers. She had to get out, had to get away. She wasn't needed any more. She didn't belong.

'What are you doing?' Daniel grated from the doorway of the room next to Josh's.

'Going back to Levos,' she told him through thin lips, stuffing the holdall with her clothes.

She heard him close the door behind him and step towards her.

'I told you, Tara is all right and in good hands. You are needed here—'

'Yes, *needed*!' she exploded in a croaky whisper, the horrors of the day rising inside her and engulfing her with pain and anguish. 'Not wanted but needed. There's a world of difference, you know—but then perhaps you don't; perhaps you are so blinded with concern for your son you can't even distinguish between right and wrong.' Her trembling hand came up and indicated the room next door. 'What you did just now was wrong, Daniel, very wrong. You led that sick boy to believe I was his mother and I'm not and...and I never will be—'

'You will be.'

'He was delirious and didn't know what he was saying—'

'He was not delirious.'

'You can't lie to children, you can't cheat them,' she sobbed.

'No one is cheating anyone.'

She threw the holdall at him then and crumpled to the bed in floods of tears, burying her face in her hands. 'You cheated me and...and you are cheating Josh. Simone should be here, not me.'

He took her in his arms but she struggled, beating her clenched fists on his chest till she was weak with the exertion.

'Go on,' he murmured. 'Punish me till you have no strength left. I deserve it for cheating you.'

She stopped, the strength draining from her, her fists still balled but suddenly useless.

'You admit it, then,' she said hoarsely, her eyes green pools of pain. 'You rat, you admit it—'

'I'm at fault, darling. I've failed miserably in not convincing you of my love for you. If that's cheating, I'm guilty.'

She tried to focus her tear-filled eyes on his face. Love? He'd said he loved her?

Suddenly she pulled away from him, her heart tearing. She got to her feet, trembling from head to toe but battling to stay stable and strong enough to speak.

'Oh, no, Daniel Kennedy. You don't love me; you never have. You used me...because of Josh. It was all for Josh and still is for Josh.'

'And didn't I accuse you of the same thing?' he challenged, getting to his feet to face her. 'Didn't I suggest that you had loved me because of Josh?'

'I didn't love you because of Josh. I loved you for you—'

Her voice gave out and she bit her lip, the realisation of what she had said slapping her in the face. Her face crumpled and she turned blindly away but he caught her and held her hard against him.

'Oh, darling. I've loved you for ever. I wanted to get you to that island on our own to tell you all I felt inside. I was angry when you refused to go, throwing Simone at me the way you did. Then I realised just how terribly insecure you were, putting up the barriers, defending yourself from hurt.'

He tilted her chin to gaze down into her eyes, which were misty pools of distress. 'Karis, I love you and want you in my life. I need you too, not for Josh, for me, because I can't bear the thought of life without you.'

Oh, she wanted to believe him. How easy it should be to close those doubts away but her insecurity went so deep. Somehow Simone's cruel words had only emphasised what she had been thinking herself—that Daniel had used her to win his son's love back. She had done that for him. He had his son's love but now Josh had been taken ill and she was needed again.

She stepped back from him, hesitant, still unsure. Trying so desperately to get it all straight in her mind.

'I...I feel trapped,' she admitted nervously. She stepped further back. 'No, don't touch me, Daniel,' she implored. She lifted her chin and looked at him, her eyes swimming with tears. 'How can I be sure, you see? I'm thinking now about that wonderful night on the beach, how you worked so hard to make it right for me. It was beautiful. The most wonderful night of my life. Everything we have done together—swimming, diving, the pirates' island... Everything—everything was wonderful, but all for...for Josh.'

Daniel shook his dark head. 'Karis, we didn't make love for Josh,' he reasoned softly.

Her mouth dropped open. No, Josh had never been in their minds then. Just him and her and the long, sensual, tropical nights.

'I...I know,' she breathed tremulously, 'but... Oh, I don't know. So many other things. Simone said—'

'When have you spoken with Simone?' he asked darkly.

Karis pushed her hair back from her face, a nervous reaction. She wasn't a sneak, telling tales. She had said too much already.

'Karis, tell me. It's important to us. I want to know everything that is troubling you.'

She bit her lip, then forced the words out because she wanted to be rid of them.

'She...she stopped me coming after you back at Fiesta's,' she whispered, eyes averted from his. 'Said I wasn't needed any more, that you had used me.' Bravely she lifted her head to look at him. 'I saw you with her, her holding your arm and you agreeing with her that she was right and you blamed yourself.'

'I *was* blaming myself, Karis. If we hadn't gone to the island at my insistence Josh might not have been sick. The rest I don't remember because I was more concerned for Josh.' He stepped towards her and held his hands out to prove he wouldn't touch her, both knowing any physical contact might cloud their reasoning. 'You didn't take the word of a scorned woman, did you?'

'She was scorned because of me, Daniel,' she insisted, 'and because she was so cruel she...she must love you and I don't feel good about that.'

'She doesn't love me, Karis. It would have been a marriage of convenience; they do exist, you know, and they can work too, if there are no outside influences. If Simone was spiteful to you it wasn't because she loves me and lost me to you; it's more a loss of prestige for her. She couldn't love Josh and he couldn't love her and she'll feel a failure for that. You're the success with Josh and she the failure.'

Karis shook her head and tried to smile. 'And because of

that you want me more than you want her. No, don't deny it, Daniel; let me finish. I loved Josh before I loved you and, you see, that is the difference between you and me.' She drew a long breath. 'You say you love me but I'll never know the truth; I'll never know if...if you love me because of Josh, be—because you want to make it right for him.'

He looked at her, his eyes unwavering; for a long, long time he looked at her. And then he spoke, words that chilled her to the very bone.

'And you never will know, Karis.'

He moved then, went to the window and moved the blinds so he could look out into the dark night. Karis felt the chill of his words and the chill of the air-conditioning and knew it was all hopeless.

'You see,' he breathed, and Karis lifted her head to look at him but he wasn't looking at her, he was gazing out into that secret world of his where she had never belonged, 'Josh loves you and you accept it because it is unconditional love; love given by a child always is. You love him back because of his love for you. I wonder if you would be quite so fond of him if he was still rejecting you?'

Karis gasped with shock. 'That's unfair!'

'But true, Karis. At the time you needed him as much as he needed you. You had a common bond. It worked for you both. Now you are willing to break that bond because of your love for me.' He turned then and faced her confused expression. 'I now know you love me very deeply. Karis; how deeply I've only just realised tonight. You don't know it yourself but you love me more than Josh. You are willing to give him up, you see, and you will have to give him up if you refuse to accept my love. You are willing to give him up because you can't believe that I can love you and want you for yourself.'

She shook her head. She didn't understand.

'And that problem is yours, Karis,' he told her thickly. 'You see, I don't have your doubts about my love. I know I love you but no amount of reasoning on my part will convince you that I want you in my life for me and not Josh.'

'Th—that's what you meant when you said I never will know?' she asked hopefully.

He shrugged. 'Karis, I can say I love you and want you in my life till I'm blue in the face but if your heart isn't open to me you will never know for sure.'

He took a deep breath and came towards her. She flinched, terrified he would touch her and she would fall into his arms and beg for some sort of salvation from what he had just given her to live with. A damning condemnation of her lack of faith and trust in him.

'I'm going out for a walk,' he told her, and she realised his tone was cold and bereft of any feeling, his way of blocking out the hurt she had inflicted on him.

She lay on the bed after he had gone, coiled in the foetal position, hugging herself for comfort. He was wrong; her heart was open, wide open and hurting so very badly. It was hurting for him and for herself. And why was she putting herself through such grief? Because of Aiden, because he had undermined her so? Daniel wasn't Aiden. Daniel was the only man she had ever truly loved; this pain she was experiencing was testimony to that.

Aiden had hurt her that night, rejected her so cruelly because of her pregnancy, but it was nothing, nothing to this agony of loss and despair she felt as she let Daniel slip away from her. Aiden was gone, a sad memory, nothing more. Daniel could never be a memory. He was so deeply ingrained in her heart he was there for this life and the next. He *was* her life and he would be gone from it if she didn't...open up her heart to him.

Later she sat up and took the little sapphire ring from the drawer of the cabinet next to the bed, her eyes soft and luminous as she gazed down at it with joy. It, like him, was beautiful, so very precious. She looked around the clinical room with its pale grey walls, blinds and metal-framed beds and smiled. It was a hell of a room to get engaged to be married in, she thought as she slipped the ring on the third finger of her left hand. It fitted perfectly, as if made for her.

She knew he would be next door with Josh. He wouldn't have walked far from his son.

He was sitting holding Josh's hand and looked up when she opened the door. Karis smiled and stood behind his chair and wafted her left hand in front of his face. She bent and whispered in his ear, 'I went ahead and did it myself.'

With a deep sigh he let go of his son's hand and took hers and pressed the ring to his warm mouth. Eventually he stood up and took her in his arms and kissed her waiting lips, a kiss so deep and passionate with promise she knew she was forgiven.

At last they drew apart and Daniel smiled adoringly at her.

'It never was meant as an engagement ring,' he murmured. 'Just a promise of something better and more exotic to come.'

'Oh,' she breathed, holding him and smiling up at him. 'Like what?'

'A diamond as big as a star.'

'This will do for me,' she told him softly. 'I'm too wild and unkempt for diamonds as big as stars. Anyway, I prefer the real thing. Stars in a velvety sky with a moon lighting them up.'

He kissed the tip of her nose. 'As I said before, it was my mother's ring. The only thing I have left of her. I've always carried it, since childhood. I've waited a lifetime to give it to the woman I love. No one else has ever worn it,' he added meaningfully.

And Karis knew that he meant Josh's mother but she didn't want confirmation. She didn't need it. She knew he loved her.

'You're kissing,' came a small voice from the bed.

Daniel and Karis, arms around each other, turned to the little boy and smiled down at him.

'Yes, son,' Daniel said tenderly. 'And you had better get used to it because you are going to see plenty more in your lifetime.'

Josh went back to sleep with a happy smile on his face.

A week later Daniel drew Karis into his arms. It was dark and rain tipped over the cottage in Levos. No moon, no stars but their passion lightened the tropical night. A passion they'd had to curtail in the hospital room in Castries till Josh was well and ready to leave.

Now, just as the rains flooded the island, they flooded themselves with their love. Passionate arousal, wanting and needing each other so much, moving together, loving each other till dawn.

'And I'll still be here in the morning when Josh and Tara come rushing in,' Daniel told her finally, clasping her love-sated body to his.

Karis laughed softly and pressed her warm lips to his neck. 'You'd better be,' she murmured happily. 'And you'd better hurry up and make it legal because Saffron is already making me a wedding dress.'

'Oh, no,' groaned Daniel, and it was the last thing he said before slipping into a deep sleep of exhaustion.

And before she slipped away herself Karis gathered her thoughts together and dwelled happily on them. Fiesta was organising their wedding on the island. Just themselves and Josh and Tara and the staff—a quiet wedding, she had promised, but Karis knew better. She wondered how her parents would cope with a wild Caribbean wedding party. Daniel had insisted they fly out, saying that it was time they bit on their stiff upper lips and realised they had grandparental responsibilities.

She knew it would be all right when they arrived. Daniel would make sure it was, just as he made sure everything was all right.

'I love you, darling,' she breathed against his warm skin. He moaned softly and tightened his hold on her and she knew he hadn't heard but that he knew all the same.

EPILOGUE

'THERE they are!' Josh cried from the rail of the yacht as they approached the jetty at Levos. Tara pushed him aside to get a better look. Josh gripped her hand tightly to stop her trying to climb the rail. 'Look, Tara, Grandpa and Grandma too. They come every year to join us. Mummy said they used to be ever so grumpy but they aren't any more. And there's Fiesta. Wave to her, Tara.'

'We have a new brother,' Josh shouted at Saffron who was waving a red bandanna from the beach.

'They know that,' Daniel laughed, standing behind him with his arm around Karis who was cradling six-month-old baby Jacob in her arms.

'What they don't know is there's another following close behind,' Karis muttered under her breath. She was two months pregnant again.

Daniel squeezed her shoulder. 'I wish I knew what the devil was causing it,' he teased, and then he turned to her. 'Do you mind?'

She grinned up at him happily. 'I want a football team.'

'Baseball,' he corrected her. 'And I think we'll soon have to think in terms of a nanny.'

'Oh, yes, some wild, unkempt person for you to fall in love with? Not if I can help it.' She laughed.

'Christ, I love you,' he breathed, and kissed her full on the lips.

'Daddy,' Josh wailed, turning to his father and frowning with disapproval. 'Saffron will hear you swearing.'

'Thank goodness we didn't persuade her to come to Florida with us,' Daniel whispered for Karis's ears only.

'She would never leave Levos, Daniel. And you compromising by us coming down here for three months of the year proves you love her as much as we do.' Karis laughed.

Daniel breathed deeply. 'It's good to be back,' he said happily, and Karis smiled and leaned her head on his shoulder.

And as Leroy hurried along the jetty to greet them and unload their mountain of luggage Karis reflected on that first time she had seen Daniel, standing at the same rail on this very boat. Stiff and unyielding, not wanting to be here, dreading meeting his son again, dreading yet more rejections. They were inseparable now. Father and son, bonded for evermore.

Karis went to clasp her wonderful husband's hand in her own but unfortunately it was already occupied by two warm little hands—Josh's and Tara's. Karis sighed happily as Leroy's brother enthusiastically started up the steel band to welcome them ashore. Soon Jacob's little hand would be slipping into Daniel's, then another's, boy or girl, she didn't mind, and nor did Daniel. And she didn't mind one little bit that Daniel Kennedy's hands were full now because later when the children were all asleep they would be full of her.

He did it every time they came here, always on the first night. He did what a man had to do. Her wonderful husband would sneak Fiesta's best china and crystal and silver out of the plantation house for that amazingly romantic barbecue on the beach. And they would drink champagne and eat mouth-watering steaks and then he would roll her around in the surf and...well, do what a man had to do.

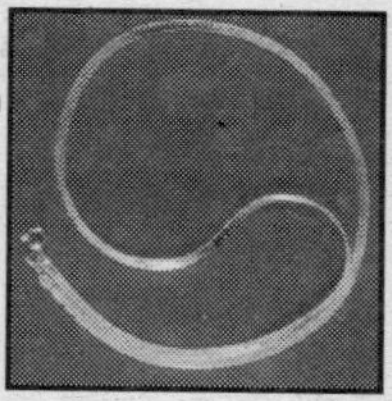